The Last Odd Day

Center Point
Large Print

**This Large Print Book carries the
Seal of Approval of N.A.V.H.**

The Last Odd Day

LYNNE HINTON

Center Point Publishing
Thorndike, Maine

For
Robin Townsley-Arcus,
who bravely sought the truth,
and for
Sharon Hinton Bender,
more than my sister,
my friend.

This Center Point Large Print edition
is published in the year 2004 by arrangement with
HarperSanFrancisco, a division of HarperCollins Publishers.

Copyright © 2004 by Lynne Hinton.

All rights reserved.

The text of this Large Print edition is unabridged. In other
aspects, this book may vary from the original edition. Printed in
Thailand. Set in 16-point Times New Roman type.

ISBN 1-58547-504-1

Library of Congress Cataloging-in-Publication Data

Hinton, J. Lynne.
   The last odd day / Lynne Hinton.--Center Point large print ed.
      p. cm.
   ISBN 1-58547-504-1 (lib. bdg. : alk. paper)
      1. Widows--Fiction. 2. Cherokee women--Fiction. 3. Loss (Psychology)--Fiction.
   4. Female friendships--Fiction. 5. Inheritance and succession--Fiction. 6. Large type books.
   I. Title.

PS3558.I457L37 2004b
813'.54--dc22
                                                                    2004008627

1

Even if the phone hadn't rung at all, the date itself is memorable because Peter Jennings on *ABC World News Tonight* had said it was the last completely odd day until the year 3111. Month, day, and year, all odd numbers, and it wouldn't happen again for another millennium.

Maude, the neighbor across the street, however, was the one who figured out things weren't right. She was the one who saw the unusual chain of events beginning to take shape; and even though she couldn't name what was coming, she certainly warned me that something out of the ordinary was on its way. She did that hours before ABC reported it, hours before the call.

She met me outside at the driveway when I went out to pick up the morning paper. She's usually up long before I am anyway since I'm accustomed to second-shift hours; and she always comes out to greet me even though she knows I'm not a morning person. That day she ran all the way out to her mailbox, her hair already combed and sprayed.

"I had one of my dreams," she said, all breathless and excited.

"What's that?" I asked, trying to pull my robe together to keep out the chill and Maude's unwanted comments about still being in my pajamas.

"My dreams," she said, walking across the street to meet me. "I had a water dream and you were in it." She

5

looked at me, and I knew she was thinking I stayed in the bed much too long. "It's about you. Your water was troubled."

Now most people consider Maude slightly irregular. She lets homeless people stay in her house. She wanted to invite a psychic woman who read tarot cards to speak to the women's circle at her church. She has seven cats, all yellow and white. And she claims she can predict disorder and upcoming unlikely events based upon dreams she has that consist of bodies of water. I don't know how she knows where the chaos will be or who it will affect, something about seeing the stirred water at a particular identifying location. Regardless of her process of interpretation, she never hesitates to announce what it is she believes is coming in your direction.

"It was green and brown. Definitely troubled," she added with a dramatic touch.

I rolled my eyes and bent down to pick up the paper. "Good morning, Maude."

"Are you up to date on your insurance policy?" Now she was standing right in front of me. She smelled like pine.

"You burning leaves?" I asked and glanced over in her yard.

"No." We had turned around and were walking together toward my house. I guessed she would be coming in for coffee. "It's an old remedy for sinus prob-lems—boiling pine straw, then sticking them in the foot of an old pair of hose and tying it onto the water faucet in the bathtub."

Maude had lots of recipes for ailments and treatments.

"You got sinus problems?"

"Always this time of year. It's the goldenrod. Mr. Thaler has it growing at the fence. I try to get him to pull it, but I think he enjoys seeing me suffer." She is short and has to walk twice as fast to keep up with me, even in the morning.

"Then maybe you need to make sure your policy is up to date." I opened the door and she walked in.

"Oh, no need to worry for me. I took out an extra policy, even with what I got from Arrow. I got coverage for everything." She went right over to the cabinet and pulled out a mug, the one with the cow in the middle, and poured herself a cup of coffee. She had worked at the local rubber factory most of her life.

"You got any milk?"

I pointed over to the refrigerator with my chin and poured myself a cup and sat down at the table.

"You know, you really should clean out these drawers down here at the bottom. You can get poison from the mold that grows on this cheese." She found the milk, checked the date on the side of the carton, and poured almost half a cup in her coffee. "Clarence Tupper had to be hospitalized because of something he ate that had been in his refrigerator too long," she added.

"Clarence Tupper was in the hospital because he weighs four hundred pounds. There ain't nothing that stays in his refrigerator too long." I unfolded the paper and began poring over the news.

Maude moved near the table and sat down next to me.

"I'm serious, Jean," she said, and she pulled the paper

away from my face. "Something grave is about to happen."

I glared at her, then snapped the paper back so that I could finish reading the front-page headlines and the temperature and weather forecast in the top right corner.

"Cold front's moving across the Piedmont." I thought I could change the subject. "You already brought your porch plants in?"

"Did that three weeks ago when the first frost came. Cats eat the leaves off my geraniums every year; they'd probably last longer outside."

I took a sip and kept reading. There had been a fire in an apartment on the other side of town.

"Maybe it's O.T."

I heard a chair being pulled out across from me, but I didn't move the paper to see exactly where she was sitting.

"He has been in there a long time."

I still didn't say anything.

"Jean Witherspoon, are you listening to me?"

I dropped the paper and sighed. "Yes, Maude, I am listening to you. You had a water dream and it's about me and you think O.T. could be dying."

"Well?" She wrapped the coffee mug with both hands and bowed her head while she kept her eyes on me.

"Well what?" I folded the paper and placed it on the table. Maude was not going to let this go.

"Well, aren't you going to call the nurse and make sure he's okay?"

I took a sip of my coffee and thought about scrambling an egg for breakfast.

"Maude, if O.T. has died, somebody would have called me. It's a policy at Sunhaven. When a patient dies, they call the family. I checked on O.T. last night. He was eating Ritz crackers and giving the nursing assistant hell because he thought the guy was trying to steal bait off his fishing pole."

I took a breath and breathed it out slowly, trying not to hurt Maude's feelings. "If there's mud in my water, it hasn't settled enough to change the current. Everything is fine."

I got up and took the skillet out of the cabinet. Then I walked to the refrigerator, making Maude slide way over in her chair so I could open the door and pull out the eggs and butter.

"You want an egg?"

Maude appeared hurt that I had not taken her counsel. She slid back in her chair, shook her head, and drank her coffee. She put the mug down, keeping her eyes on the table.

"Maude, I'll call after I eat."

She nodded without looking at me. "These dreams," she said without lifting her head, "they're such a burden." She paused for a minute. "Everybody wants to be special, but it isn't everything you think it will be."

I cracked open the egg and dropped it in a bowl, whipped it around with some salt and pepper, and poured it in the skillet, which was already hot and popping.

"Yeah, I guess all the prophets must have had some bad days." My back was toward her. "At least you don't have to tell the king that God is pissed and that the sky

9

is going to rain fire." I lowered the heat. "Or locusts and frogs," I added. "At least locusts aren't in your dreams."

I turned around to face her, show her a little more sympathy; and Maude was reading my paper. She wasn't as hurt as I thought. I turned to the stove and finished cooking my egg. By the time I was done and had buttered my toast and set my plate on the table, Maude had fixed herself a bowl of cereal and was reading the astrology section. We finished our breakfasts in silence.

"Well, I have to run to the bank. It looks like today is my best day of the month to make those financial transactions. Call me later when you hear from O.T." Then she hurried out the door with a wave of her fingers and the birdcall she always uses for good-bye, "Tootledoo."

I shook my head and finished reading the news. Then I cleaned up the dishes and examined what was in the refrigerator, deciding that my meddlesome neighbor was right about one thing: the cheese had to go. And once I decided to pitch it, I filled my arms with other bags and containers bearing items I didn't even recognize.

I was trying to pull the trash can out from under the sink with my foot when the phone started to ring. After trying to negotiate the food and the cabinet without any success, I dropped the stuff in the sink and grabbed the phone on the fourth ring. It was too late, as the machine was already giving the message.

"Just hang on!" I shouted.

"Hello? Hello?" I heard the voice on the other end.

"Just wait a minute." The message was almost finished. Finally the beep sounded, and since I couldn't get

10

to the machine in the den, it was recording the conversation.

"Hello?" I said.

"Uh, yes, hello." The voice seemed hesitant. A woman's voice. Young, I thought. "Is this the Oliver Witherspoon residence?"

"Sort of." I replied. "Who's calling?"

There was a pause. I heard her breathe.

"Is Oliver Witherspoon there?" Her voice sounded tight, stretched across some depth of feeling—fear, anxiety, I couldn't tell for sure.

"Oliver Witherspoon is my husband. Can I help you?"

Another pause. Then the beep on the machine sounded and it cut off.

"I need to speak to Oliver Witherspoon."

"Well, he isn't here." I was thinking it was some marketing person, somebody from over at the tractor place in Raleigh, where he bought all his machinery. They called every year even though I told them he was not buying any new farm equipment.

"Do you know what time he'll return?"

I hesitated. I didn't like giving out information about our situation to strangers over the phone. "Look, if you'll tell me who you are and why you're calling, I'll be happy to let Mr. Witherspoon know."

There was a click, and the phone went dead. She hung up.

O.T. had been at Sunhaven Nursing Home almost seventeen months when she made the first contact. Since the massive brain hemorrhage and the broken hip, the feeding tube and the ministrokes, I could no longer take

11

care of him by myself. He required constant attention, and even with bringing in a sitter for a few hours every day, I could not manage him alone.

I acted on the doctor's strictest advice, received many reassurances from those who understood, but none of that took away the sting of what I chose to do. Taking him to that place was the hardest decision I had made in more than thirty-seven years of marriage. It kept me up at nights, aged me, depleted me. It made me wish that I was dead.

Of course if you knew us, knew us well, you would be confused at that final number because O.T. and I were married more than fifty-five years. Count it up and you would realize that sometime during the first fifteen to twenty years of our matrimony I had made another difficult choice. You might then cluck your tongue to the roof of your mouth, nod knowingly, a nervous smile, and only wonder, or maybe, if you're nosy like my neighbor Maude, not afraid to ask the obvious, you'd want me to tell you about the other decision.

Now not such a long time ago, I would have said in carefully chosen words or discreet body language, a quick retreat from your presence, to mind your own business; but since I am now a woman who no longer hides much of anything, a woman unafraid to open up her closet and parade her skeletons in front of any audience, I would more than likely oblige.

"Ask me a question," I would say to you. "But do not be offended if the answer I give is more information than you would like."

After fifteen years and eleven months of being O.T.'s

wife, I walked out for forty-six days. I left him until I decided whether or not to stay married, whether or not to stay myself. I packed up most of everything I owned, which I could fit into the trunk of our Mercury, drove down to Wrightsville Beach, rented a room at the Ocean View Motel, and listened to the steady crash and pull of the ocean as it crested and fell, just like the contents of my heart.

Late on a Friday morning in November, just like the one when Lilly called, I cleaned out my closet, the drawers in the bureau, the shelves above the toilet, and one small corner of the kitchen hutch where I kept my grandmother's china, put everything in boxes and plastic bags and two large suitcases, turned the car east, and drove until the pavement ran out. Right at the entrance of the Ocean View Motel. And there I stayed until I could finally cry.

When I finished weeping and awoke from the death sleep I fell into afterward, both of them feeling like they would last forever, I repacked the suitcases, the bags, and the boxes, paid my bill, and came home. It seemed to neighbors and friends that it was only a needed vacation, that I had rested and eased; but I knew better. I knew that I had made a choice, a choice that kept my life in motion, a choice to take in air and let it out, a choice to survive even if the deeper things were not changed.

It would be a moment, a choice, that kept my heart beating, my marriage and life in order. And on I would go like this for almost forty years until there would be another agonizing decision to make. More than thirty-seven years before O.T. got out of his restraints and fell out of his bed. Thirty-nine years and eleven months before the phone call.

Right up until the moment I was forced to make this second major decision, I was picking him up and carrying him to his room, still thinking that I could do anything. But after that spill and the consequential fracture in his hip, the dull ache down in the bottom of my spine, the way my hands couldn't stop shaking, I knew my abilities to care for him were lessening and then finally limited. Once we made it to the hospital I scheduled my first appointment with Sunhaven. I cried the entire time.

I believed for a very long time that I had failed him, that I should have been able to keep him at home. But after the choice was made, just like the one at the beach, I stayed with it, learned to let it be. And I suppose if anybody is keeping score, two major life decisions in fifty-five years wouldn't be such an awful record. There are certainly worse lives to lead than mine.

The phone rang three more times during the day on November 19, 1999. Each time I answered Lilly hung up. Finally, at 9:33 p.m. when I was wiping up the table from where I had been cutting up apples to freeze, the phone rang again. Without a proper greeting, I spoke.

"Oliver Witherspoon is a resident at Sunhaven Nursing Home. I suggest that if you're looking to speak only to him, you make a visit since he does not take phone calls."

Then I was the one to hang up. It would be three more months before I would hear from her again.

2

On the surface, if you'd seen my parents in passing, they appeared mismatched, poorly yoked, all wrong for each other. You likely would have dismissed their marriage, crossed your brow in disapproval. You would have thought that something was not right about the two of them being together.

However, what I learned of love and marriage came swiftly and gently from the relationship I witnessed between them. Though our time together as family was brief and even laden with sorrow, here is the place where I learned how good it can really be.

John Clover Andrews was white-skinned and gray-haired, twenty years older than my mother. He was blind and weak-natured, prone to nightmares and frightening premonitions. My mother, Mary Whitebead, was young with a dark complexion and disposition. She was Cherokee and Navajo, brown and sullen, strong in will and composition, quiet with eyes calmed from disappointment.

You would have taken one glance at them and passed a quick judgment, believing that surely they were all wrong for each other. That's if you had seen them just out of the corner of your eye. But if you had taken a few minutes and followed, quietly watching them as one stood near the other, and saw the way my mother softened and my father bloomed, you would have seen clearly how right it was that they were husband and wife.

If you had taken just a little time and studied how they melted into each other, how they flowed together, one beginning where the other ended, two streams now a river, you would have understood. The force of their union would have persuaded you.

It defeated any doubt. The two of them together, married and in love, is one of the few things in life of which I have been certain.

My mother said she loved my father because he knew her through hearing her, through feeling her, loved the way she was at the tip of his fingers, the way he touched her sorrow and did not retreat. She loved him because he was not interested in how her body curved or how her eyes flashed, how she appeared walking across a room. She knew his love grew from inside his heart.

She claimed she was drawn to him because he bore the soul of a woman; he was not ashamed to cry. He said he loved her because she was not afraid of silence and because she smelled of chicory and buttonbush flowers. He loved her because she had an uncanny way of letting things be, that he knew her to be as old as the mountain upon which we lived.

They stumbled upon each other late on a summer evening when he walked in the direction of the haunting call of a horned owl. John Clover was standing near a stream, just in the curve at the side of the hill where wildflowers grew tall and unbothered. He stood, alone and satisfied in the dark because at night he felt undamaged and whole. He followed the sound because he believed it was leading him, steering him toward some destiny; and when he fell upon my mother, asleep in the jewelweed, he was confident that she had been waiting for him.

Mary had wandered into the woods, down from the mountain where she lived, to spend the night, to rest between the roots of box elders and sugarberry trees, to lie upon the warm earth and feel its pulse. When my father came upon her, having tripped on a stone near where she lay, my mother was dreaming that she was weaving strands of grass, bending and folding them into the perfect basket, that her fingers became the golden pieces of straw and that she was being pulled into something strong and fast. When she awoke and heard the breath of the man sitting near her, behind a rock, listening but not watching, she too believed he came to her to tighten the strings around her heart.

Neither family was particularly happy. Lives were threatened, tears spilled. Bloodlines were broken and battle lines drawn. But my mother, labored and delivered into sadness, searching only for someone who would not pull her from it, and my father, blinded by love and dependent on someone who could tell him the colors of a storm cloud, would not be denied.

They slipped away farther into the hills, were married by a shaman and later a circuit-riding minister, and returned to claim ten acres of his great-grandfather's stolen property, her ancestors' burial land. And there, edged by the graves of those who died and were thought to have rested, they built a house on the far corner of the acreage and a new life together for themselves.

That is where we lived, my parents and me and long, roaming spirits in search of peace and two distinct but

17

intersected histories, old and young, Indian and white. Over the years I came to understand that they are both equally and uniformly me.

I was born November 15, 1927, another odd day, in my parents' bedroom late in the afternoon. I was their second child, the middle one, hoped for but unexpected, the one who lived. Bennie Whitestream was their first, named for the men who had presided at their weddings; and he died several years before I was born. He was seven months old, thin and rickety like my father, silent and pensive like my mother.

Aunt Carolyn said it was cholera, that it had taken more than one baby from a mother's arms but that Bennie's death was even more difficult since my mother did not tell anyone for thirteen days that he had died. Daddy knew something had happened. The baby, who had been crying for almost a month, was quiet; and my mother, while burning heavy incense, stayed in a rocking chair, her back to the door for almost two weeks. He tried to get her to talk to him, tried to take Bennie from her, but Mama would not let him near her or the baby, repeating to him to go away, to stay out of the room, and that everything was fine.

Finally, even though Daddy was blind and incapable, he hitched up the horse and drove the wagon into a town three counties over, returning with the doctor and the preacher, who ultimately forced her to let the baby go.

Her sister-in-law claimed the baby had been dead for more than just a few days, that the little body was stiff and blue, and that when they pried my brother out of my grieving mother's arms the stench almost knocked those three grown men to the floor.

Mama never seemed to notice; and in fact when I finally did hear this story from my aunt as she walked with me to our house after Mama's funeral, I remembered how the old Indian women always cut sagebrush and waved the burning sticks around themselves when Mama came near. She would cut her eyes at them and say they were just acting crazy, but I later figured out that they could still smell my brother's passing on her breath. His death had melted inside her chest like boiled glaze on a cake, and even years and years afterward, she carried him on her like a bundle of blankets tied around her heart.

When my sister Emma died, Aunt Carolyn and the others said Mama did much better. She did not fast or weep. She was cooperative and forthcoming. She wrapped my sister in her grandmother's quilt and took her to the clearing behind the house where other family members and her ancestors were buried. There hadn't even been time for a grave opening. But she sat there on a stump, waiting, rocking her dead child until the men came with a pine box, the preacher arrived and said a few words, and my daddy and his brothers were able to dig a hole fast and wide.

I watched from behind a tree as she willfully laid her daughter in the coffin and even helped nail it shut. I was surprised at her ease with it all even without knowing about Bennie. But I guess she was so weary of death and resigned to the whims of God, she just accepted that to balance out the suffering on the mountain, one more child of hers had to be taken.

She was always talking about the pain up there in the hills, how the young ones never knew the torture that occurred on the long walk to Oklahoma, which was deeper and longer than the one shown on maps. It was, she had said, a truly groaning path that etched its way alongside the mountain, deep in its valleys, and within the veins of every Indian.

Mama was born within a small segment of the nation that had managed to escape the Indian Removal Act of 1830, which forced all the Native Americans of the southeastern United States to move west. Particularly harsh for the Cherokee, the U.S. government sent more than seven thousand troops into the territory, pushing the people away from their homes without any warning or time to prepare.

She would tell the story stone-eyed and quietly of how the soldiers had pulled her great-grandmother from her home, forced her away without any of her belongings and without even knowing where her children or husband were. They ransacked and pillaged, even destroying the sacred resting grounds, so sure they were that gold was hidden among the ruins.

My mother's great-grandmother buried herself in a pile of leaves, and listened for the sounds of her children as the whole community, aimless and broken, wandered by. She finally recognized the cries of her baby son and daughter and reached up from the ground, pulling them down with her. They stayed there, the old story goes, for more than a day waiting for the sounds of her husband, their father, until finally the soldiers and all of the other Indians had passed. Then without any word from my mother's great-grandfather, they fled deep into the mountains where a few other Cherokee had hidden out.

My great-great-grandmother never found her husband though she listened for him every day until she died. Everyone says she claims that she heard his spirit along with all the others who had been captured or killed that dreadful day calling out their dying whispers in the wind that poured down from the hill. Every autumn, in a prayerful and learned manner, my mother would turn toward the tallest mountain and say words I did not understand.

"They still speak," she would say, her voice choked and small. "They still call out from *oosti ganuhnuh dunaclohiluh.*"

Later I would find the words she pronounced in a book in the small library Dr. Hughes had built for the school. *Oosti ganuhnuh dunaclohiluh:* it means the trail where they cried.

In a perfect twist of irony, my daddy's great-grandfather was one of the settlers from farther south who moved onto my mother's people's land. They came up and staked off a hundred acres, claiming it was open territory and theirs for the taking. The Georgia women begged to go home because their crops failed and because the family was plagued with illness and melancholy, the land seeded in sorrow. But the men would not be moved. They remained convinced that they belonged to the land and that the land belonged to them, convinced that Indian gold was somewhere up in those hills and that it would all be theirs. They would not leave the mountain. Even God would not turn them away.

I believe that just like my mother, my father wrestled with his family's history, with the evil that was done by those in his lineage, by those whose lines led down to him. I never asked and he never spoke of how he measured their sins. He never mentioned his parents or grandparents.

Sometimes though, late in the afternoon, when the mountain was brushed in sunlight, shimmering in hot, brilliant streams of yellow, he would ask as if he were trying to make sense of something, a thread of sadness in his voice, "Does it seem to be made of gold?"

My mother would always answer graciously. "Yes," she would say, pretending it didn't hurt, "it bears the glimmer of dreams."

My father would nod slowly, as if he understood.

Somehow, watching, listening from my bedroom window, I was reminded of how their marriage, just as that brief conversation, always felt to me like so much more than the words that were spoken, so much more than what was visible just on the surface.

The question, the answer, the way they loved each other, the way they bore one another's grief, the way it was between them, without everything always having to be said out loud and with witnesses, these things always felt to me like prayer.

3

Winter in North Carolina, two hours east of the Blue Ridge Parkway and the Appalachian Ridge, is like a new wife. Neither demanding nor harsh, she is a season of submission, a lovely opportunity to create the illusion that the world is a perfect place. She is easy and mild, the period that lulls you into a false sense that little to no maintenance is required. Then when the husband has grown accustomed to fresh baking smells in the kitchen and passionate surprises in the bedroom, when he is used to wearing no coat and leaving the windows opened, suddenly there is a brutal blast and the sky changes colors and a storm snaps power lines and brings any movement to a halt.

Women more than men, I have noticed, hide vital information about themselves from the one they promise to love. It is an old trick handed down from mother to daughter, an ancient tool of survival that says in subtle hints, "Pay attention to this!"

It is as if we learn that what we have is not acceptable and that if we are found out, the cat discovered and let out of the bag, we will be left abandoned and ashamed. So that even after years of courting, intimate conversations, and private moments, there are still secrets we do not share. We marry in hopes that the secrets will be consumed by the fire of our love and the ashes buried by vows of fidelity and our sincere longing to please one man.

We start out with a grand twisting of desire and romance, actually believing that we can guess what a husband needs even before hearing it and that we are capable of fulfilling every craving he might have. We spend hours, days, weeks scheming and planning to make him surprised and happy that he would have picked such a mate, such a woman as I.

And for a few months, maybe even a year, we think it has worked; we believe that we have tamed the blues and hushed the relentless whisper from our hearts that says, You cannot be the thing you are not. We push and pull, starve and curse the parts of ourselves we have been told are not to be mentioned or shown; and we pray that they will not spill or sneak outside our hold.

Then a sharp crack of lightning flashes, a tiny fissure develops. There is a shifting of the low heavy clouds. He comes home and doesn't seem to appreciate enough or notice enough; and like a sudden and surprising storm of jagged, blinding pellets of ice, we freeze, paralyzing what has become familiar.

Generally, this unexpected storm of truth does not destroy the landscape or obliterate the home. It merely chills things, causes a marriage to catch its breath, the trees to bend low. Eventually everything snaps back into place. But after that first unsuspected blow of winter, no one walks about carelessly again.

O.T. and I weathered our first winter storm when he walked in on a Saturday, from the hog lot, mud on his shoes and a stupid grin on his face, and sat down at the table at a quarter after eleven expecting lunch. Never mind that I had worked my shift and three hours overtime or that I was on my way out to the grocery store to replenish what was gone.

Because of what I had been doing for nine and a half months since he had returned from overseas and because of what he had seen his mother do all his life, he just assumed a meal, hot and hearty, would greet him anytime he sat down at the table. I threw a loaf of bread,

24

the jar of mustard, and two slices of bologna at him and walked out the door, slamming it behind me. He never came in the house in quite the same way again.

The storm, fast and furious, blasted through; and from then on O.T. and I understood how quickly the sky can change. Afterward, we never took warmth or comfort for granted again. We survived, but there was a shift in the marriage.

Three months from the day after Maude had her crazy water dream about me, that day a young woman called for my husband, there was a flimsy report of potential snow flurries in central North Carolina. Since I had skidded across the road and into the side of a bridge the previous year during a bout of freezing rain and because I understood the consequences of dismissing such signs both in the weather and in relationships, I left early for Sunhaven to visit O.T.

Usually I arrived at the nursing home just after the shift change, and therefore I did not know the early staff as well as I did those who came in after 2:30 p.m. I met almost everyone when O.T. first went in because I used to go right after breakfast and stay all day; but over time I drifted into the comfortable schedule of leaving home at the same time I had for more than fifty-one years while I worked at the mill.

I slept until 10:00 a.m. By the time I was through piddling about, taking care of chores and errands, I didn't get to Sunhaven until around 3:00. I stayed until after supper, helping him eat and change for bed, and I was with him until he fell asleep. It had become our routine. So that after more than twenty months, in season and out of season, this is how we did our marriage.

I was friendly with all the nurses and nursing assistants from the afternoon shift. They became like a second family. We saw each other so often that we began to learn all sorts of things about each other; and before I knew it we were sharing intimate details of our lives and giving advice as freely as we shared recipes and gardening tips. Everyone knew O.T. as well as I did since he became a different person after the stroke. So it seemed, after a while, that they were telling me more things about him than I could share with them. They knew his favorite activity and his worst time of day. They knew what frightened him and what reassured him. And they knew what he liked to eat.

Before moving to Sunhaven, O.T. had never cared for Jell-O or pudding, called it "ladies' food," but once he moved there, it appeared he'd do anything for cherry Jell-O. Like a child hearing the threat of no allowance, O.T. performed whatever task was needed for a promise of the red food that wiggles.

It was, of course, quite a shock to discover that other women knew more about my husband than I did. I had come in for my regular visit, and Betty, the nursing assistant who lives only a couple of miles from me, was feeding him a snack.

I saw the spoon in her hand, the red cube shaking on top. "He won't eat it, Betty, he hates Jell-O."

And the next thing I know, O.T. is grinning and clapping his hands, "Ollie wants jiggly."

Betty shrugged her shoulders, trying to downplay her significance in my husband's life. "You can never tell with stroke patients, Mrs. Witherspoon, their likes and dislikes can change from one day to the next."

But I didn't let that bother me. I had left most of my ego outside the door when I brought O.T. there in the first place. And then, two weeks after he had been there and they were able to get him to drink a milkshake and finally get that awful feeding tube out of his throat, I humbly accepted that they were more qualified and better caregivers than I was.

On that cold day in February, I walked past the nurses' station and down the hall to room 117. O.T. was in the bed by the window since he liked staring outside at the bird feeder and had seniority over his roommate who had moved in only one month earlier.

I said hello to Mr. Parsons, a double amputee whose wife had only recently died and whose son lived out west and never visited. He hardly ever had anything to say.

"Hey, baby," I said as I pulled open the blinds and looked over and smiled at my husband. "Getting a little cloudy today, maybe snow." I began cleaning up around his bed, straightening papers, throwing away trash.

"Snow today," he said and nodded.

"What did you eat for breakfast?" There were large yellow stains all down the front of his pajamas. "Looks like oatmeal," I answered myself and went over to the closet and pulled out a clean shirt. "Let's get you changed." And I helped him out of the pajama top and pulled a sweatshirt over his head.

"Clara," he said as I smoothed his hair back down.

"No, baby, I'm Jean."

I balled up the stained top and put it in a plastic grocery bag I had brought to carry home his dirty laundry. I washed his clothes on Wednesdays and Fridays.

"So sorry, Jean." A tear rolled down his cheek.

After O.T. had his stroke, his personality changed. He was more volatile, more emotional, sometimes screaming for no reason, sometimes crying for hours. It was very difficult at first since O.T. was never high-strung. The most upset I ever saw him was when he pulled the tractor off his daddy and carried him all the way to the fire station, a good mile and a half from the house.

He was raw and fierce, determined to walk his father back to life. The coroner said Papa had to have died instantly, that amount of weight crushing his whole right side; but it wouldn't have mattered to O.T. even if he had known that when it happened. He was not about to put his father down until he laid him on the stretcher in the fire truck.

I yelled at him from the house, told him I'd bring the car around; but he threw his father across his shoulders and just started walking. By the time I got the keys and pulled the car out of the driveway, he was halfway across the field and farther away from me. I followed him along the road, blowing the horn and trying to get him to walk to the car. He just kept moving, until finally he stopped and in a voice that could only come from grief, he roared, "Damn it, Jean, just go to the station and tell Jimmy to meet me with the truck."

And so I did. I left my husband walking across a field of soybeans, his father, bloody and broken, slung around his shoulders, and drove down the dirt road to the fire station. Jimmy Morgan and Ellis Rumley jumped in the paramedics' truck and met him just as he was coming out of the field. And by the time I got to them O.T. had calmed down and was standing behind the two EMTs, just rubbing his neck and shaking his head. He didn't even cry at the funeral.

The time I left him to go to Wrightsville Beach, he showed up the fifth day. But after seeing me and realizing that what I mostly needed was space, he never said a word, never explained how he found me or why it took him five days. He never talked about what happened or what it was like for him.

He put some money on the table by the window in the motel room, cupped his big hand around the top of my head, pressing me to the earth, and walked out.

When I got home, he was a little more tender, a little more careful with his words; but he did not cry or twirl me around in glee, he just helped me take the bags out of the car, placed the china back in the corner of the hutch, drew me a bath, and fixed me a banana sandwich, which he fed to me as I sat in the tub.

He never, in our entire state of matrimony, ever raised his voice or became overwhelmed by emotion. Only that scream from the field of sorrow and a look in his eye when he came to the ocean that almost melted the hard shell surrounding my heart.

There at the last, seeing him cry became a normal thing. Although it was troublesome and difficult for me at first, after more than a year and a half it was just a part of who my husband had become.

"There, there, old man, there's no need to lose it over spilled oatmeal." And I wiped the tears from his eyes. "You're just having one of your sad spells."

He turned away from me and stared out the window. He nodded his head like there was nothing more to be said. "Red birds run the others off."

I noticed where he was watching the feeder. A large male cardinal was sitting on the small post that extends from the dark round opening where the seed was most plentiful.

"Fat ole thing, isn't he?"

O.T. laughed. "Who you calling fat?" And somehow through the bars of his hospital bed he was able to reach out and pinch me on the rear. He startled me.

O.T. could seem clear and normal at certain moments. He would remember names and dates, circumstances surrounding events that I had forgotten. He was at times conversational and winsome, able to tell you what he wanted or needed, when he was cold or what channel of the television he wanted to watch. And during those moments, rare as they were especially in the last months, I would think the effects of the stroke had passed, that he had been given a reprieve, a healing; and in just a blink of the eye, I was consumed by shame that I had sent him to a nursing facility and began considering what it might mean to take him home.

Those moments would quickly dissolve, however. And he would start to cry, call me Mama, or scream at somebody passing by the room. He had been permanently damaged by the stroke, a cerebrovascular accident, a thrombosis, the doctors named it; a train

30

wreck, Maude more aptly called it.

In less time than it took me to open the car door and wave hello, O.T. fell from the first step of the porch to the bottom step beside the sidewalk, deprived almost half of his brain of oxygen, and went from being a 230-pound man of such dignity and pride he wouldn't even ask for help when the tobacco came in and who could quote entire passages of Shakespeare and the Bible to being a 135-pound man who had to wear a diaper and could not understand something as simple as sucking milk through a straw.

Seeing him the way I did those last few months, an infant in a grown man's body, reduced my faith to something smaller than a mustard seed, leaving my spirit as cracked and withered as the skin on an old woman's hand. And even when I found out what he had done, the chilling realization that there was more to our marriage than what I knew, I still would never have wished such a thing as his declining condition on anyone, even and especially on him.

Karen Hertford was his nursing assistant that day. Her mother had worked with me at the mill. I remember pictures of the girl when she was only a toddler, and I recognized her last name the first time I met her when O.T. was new at Sunhaven. Her mother and I were never close friends, but we knew things about each other like the facts that she had a steel pin in her left ankle and that we both enjoyed jalapeño peppers cut and quartered and soaked in a little vinegar.

Karen had just started working at the nursing home when O.T. first came. She had a pleasant nature about her, which after more than a year and a half, I noticed, had remained intact. She was slightly overweight, pulled her hair up in a ponytail, and always kept a fine manicure.

"Well, hello, Mrs. Witherspoon, what are you doing here this time in the day?" She moved the swivel table into the curtain that separated the two beds so she could get beside O.T. "I haven't seen you since your husband was a new patient."

She pulled the blood pressure cuff down from the attachment on the wall behind O.T.'s head and added, "And how is my favorite fellow?" O.T. smiled.

"I know. I'm so used to those afternoon hours it's hard for me to change my ways." I straightened O.T.'s shirt.

"This is Jean." O.T. smiled at Karen.

"Yes, Mr. Witherspoon, I know." She wrapped the sleeve around his arm. "Did Walter help you eat your breakfast?"

"Walter's an asshole." He yanked his arm away, and Karen had to pull it toward her, brace it under her arm, and start again.

"O.T., that's not fair," I said, then, "I'm sorry," to Karen.

"Oh, no need to apologize; your husband's right. Walter is an asshole." She said it so matter-of-factly I was shocked. I had always assumed there was some rule against talking badly about the other staff.

O.T. nodded. There was a pause as she listened for the thumps that registered my husband's flow of blood.

"Well, your pressure's fine." She jerked the cuff off and put it back in its holder. The black cords dangled

32

over O.T.'s head. "Let me hold your hand now." O.T. held out his arm while Karen softly placed her fingers around his wrist. She took his pulse while she winked at him.

All the attendants babied him, flirted with him like that. At first it made him angry and I found it degrading, but then I figured it was just the way they offered care; and O.T. grew to love the possibility that he might still be a virile man, attractive to younger women. So while he was enthralled with this kind of attention, Karen stuck the thermometer in his ear and noted his temperature. I realized it was more than just a means of care giving, it was also a scheme to get his compliance.

She took out a small pad of paper and jotted down the numbers. "I hope you've been doing okay," she said.

"Just fine," I replied. "How's your mother?" I opened up the drawer in the little chest right by O.T.'s bed. I found a comb and began fixing his hair.

"She had gallbladder surgery last week, the hard kind where they cut you all the way across your belly; but she's home now and doing better." She peered out the window, "You think it's going to snow?"

I glanced outside with her. The sky appeared heavy, full and ready to split. "They sure have been calling for it," I answered. "I'd love to see a little snow."

"Yeah, me too. It's like a tonic."

"A what?" I asked.

"You know, a tonic. My grandmother used to make them for us, laxatives, moisturizers, homemade remedies to fix things." She was rolling O.T. over and changing the sheets. "Just seems like snow is a natural way to soften the steely ground, free us up of pests."

"Well that's true," I replied, thinking of my own grandmother's poultices and bottles of cream. "Without a good snow, the bugs are worse in the spring and summer."

I put the comb in the drawer. "There you are, sir, you are looking mighty fine this morning."

O.T. grinned and shook his head slightly. Karen slid the clean bottom sheet under him while pushing the dirty one toward me. I pulled it out and rolled it into a ball. While she finished with the bottom one I walked around and helped with the top sheet. I noticed that the bedsore on O.T.'s heel had closed and was not nearly so inflamed.

"Well that's a lot better."

Karen twisted his foot around so that she could see. "Yeah, that one took a lot of work. It's amazing how quickly their skin wears down; that sore came up in a day."

She went over to the closet and pulled out a slender strip of lamb's wool and cupped it around the bottom of O.T.'s foot. Then we draped the sheet over him. She checked his catheter bag and jotted down a few more notes.

"All right, sweetie," she said to my husband, "you are finally all done." She touched him on the shoulder. "I bet you and your wife will have a lot to talk about today."

I appeared a little surprised, I'm sure, since I didn't understand what she meant. O.T. and I hadn't carried on a real conversation in years. There was always more silence than discourse.

Then she added, "Because of the weather, and," she whispered this, "he made you something." And she pointed her chin toward the window, near the bottom right side.

"Oh," was all I said, and I turned and saw a red construction heart pasted on the inside of the window. Somehow I had missed it when I came in. It was a valentine card he had made with the help of the recreation director.

I walked over to it. "Ollie loves Jean" was written on the inside of the heart with broad purple strokes. I touched it and smiled at O.T.

"It's lovely, honey, thank you."

He just watched the birds.

Karen pushed the table to where it had been and stood just inside the curtain that divided the room between her two patients. "By the way, I guess you realize you just missed your daughter." She began pulling aside the blue flimsy drapes so that she could work on Mr. Parsons. "I think it's so nice that she's moved home to check on him; it must be a real comfort." Then she disappeared behind the curtain and dragged it around the tracks for privacy.

I remember that Mrs. Loflin from across the hall started yelling then. She was shouting for a nurse to help her get out of the bed and that some boy was trying to kill her. Then there was the response of someone screaming at her to hold on a minute. I remember Mr. Parsons's deep breaths as Karen was checking his lungs. An old man's sigh followed by a command of "Again." I remember the quick turning of O.T.'s head like he had heard his mother's voice. And I remember the sudden flash of red, just at the corner of my eye, a cardinal, brash and bothered, pushing the other birds away from the feeder.

It's funny the things you remember at significant moments. Colors, sounds, the reaction on somebody else's face. It's so odd how when you reflect about a particular event of revelation—a news report, a doctor's prognosis, a sudden jolt in an otherwise monotonous chain of moments—you can be so completely clear about the unimportant details that you actually have a difficult time defining the event in terms that other people can understand.

Like Mary Magdalene in the garden when they discovered Jesus' body was gone. I imagine that she would have been able to tell the other women, the disciples, things like how the flowers, tiny pink ones, were particularly redolent and how the angle of the sun had cast a shadow across a mound of stones. She could have told them how the morning dew had settled upon slender leaves, bowing them toward the ground like a child's head dropped to pray.

She would remember that her veil had fallen from across her face and that the cool breeze chilled her lips, causing her to reach up and slide her fingers across them, leaving the taste of the spices she and the others had brought and dropped when they realized someone had been to and opened the grave. Rose oil and spikenard, aloe and a hint of myrrh. And she would remember exactly where she stood when he called her name.

They would want to know things like how he seemed or where he said he had been, how it happened; but it would be the golden light in his eyes, the way he held his hands open and loose, the softness of his voice, these would be the things that came to mind.

And though Mary would never share such memories, these would be the only cues for remembering how it was when she saw a resurrected Jesus, the one she loved more than anything, life itself, dead and now alive.

Maude would ask me later, "Oh, my God, Jean, what did you do when you heard?" And I would think of the gasp and exhale of my husband's roommate, the terror from somebody's never-ending nightmare, a sudden blink of O.T.'s eyes that convinced me he knew what was about to be told, and the distracting blast of scarlet just beyond my line of vision.

O.T. closed his eyes like he was going to sleep. I started walking around him toward Mr. Parsons's side of the room. "Karen, what daughter?" I did not pull the curtain open since I knew privacy was one of the few luxuries the patients at Sunhaven only rarely were able to afford. I stood at the foot of his bed.

"Why didn't you eat anything?" She was still engaged with her patient.

He mumbled something in return. I checked O.T. He was sleeping. His brow wrinkled and fell.

"What is it, Mrs. Witherspoon?" She was coming toward me. She found the opening and walked through. She wrote down some things on the little pad she kept in the front pocket of her uniform.

"My daughter who's been visiting O.T.?" I stepped

aside so that she'd have room to stand in front of the door.

"Yeah," she spoke hurriedly, "Lilly." Then she saw that Mrs. Loflin was hanging upside down on the side of her bed. "Lord, Lucy, what have you done this time?" She ran across the hall before I could ask another question.

Mrs. Loflin had not gotten the help she wanted, so she had decided she could get out of the bed by herself. What she hadn't taken into account was the thick band of cloth tying her right arm tightly to the side rail. She had managed to undo the left restraint, but the other one was a bit too knotted for her to pull apart. She had fallen over on her head trying to release herself. I stood in the hallway while Karen managed to get her back into bed.

The only visitors I know who came to call on O.T. were Maude when she happened to be on that side of town, his youngest brother and his new wife, Beatrice, once every other week, the preacher from the Baptist Church because he visited everybody, and an occasional friend from the Rotary Club where O.T. had served as president and been a member since 1958.

No other women had ever visited my husband. We just weren't close to any. We didn't have a lot of friends. There were no nieces within a hundred miles; and even if one of them did come by they would certainly contact me since I can't believe they would be able to find this place on their own. The women I worked with and considered acquaintances were as old as I was, and most of them were taking care of their own husbands. I didn't think any of them would have time to visit, and even if they did, none of them was young enough to be my child.

I was absolutely puzzled, and I stood there in the hall waiting for Mrs. Loflin to get turned right side up so that I could find out who my daughter was. It was like trying to chase down a real person to talk to when you call the phone company. Karen went from Mrs. Loflin to Mr. Trabor, who was urinating in the corner of the hall, to a new physical therapy assistant who had put the walking belt backward on Charles Foust and was about to drop him by the linen chute. Then she hurried to the nurses' station to answer a phone call and explain why the Alzheimer's patient on the other hall needed to be moved to another room. She would keep trying to talk to me, but the interruptions were fast and furious. And I followed her around like a child.

Finally, it seemed things slowed just enough for her to stop and catch her breath. She seemed surprised to see me. "Mrs. Witherspoon, what's the matter? Does your husband need something?"

I shook my head no and saw her focusing around me at a commotion near the door of the dining room. I stood up taller, trying to block her view. "The woman you said who's been visiting O.T." I shrugged my shoulders. "Karen, we don't have any children."

She seemed confused. "Miss Thomas, quit pushing Aunt Babe," she yelled to the women behind me. Then she turned to me. "She's been coming about three months now. Said her name was Lilly, from somewhere east of here, not too far, I think."

She sighed because Aunt Babe was starting to cry.

"Every day," she added, "about the time I get here." Then she was gone. Miss Thomas had started pulling hair.

I stood there in the hallway, a crazy world spinning around me. Clouds building up on the horizon, practically bursting at the seams. People screaming for help, others moaning like they were facing death head-on, nurses and staff trying to create some semblance of order, and the news that a woman, a daughter named Lilly, had discovered my husband and was visiting him.

More than eleven weeks she had been coming. Three months. Almost ninety days. Somebody who believed herself to be family had sat near O.T. and watched him, learned him, maybe even cared for him. There had been a flood of unexplained emotions, a storm blowing through hearts, and I had not known.

4

Emma Lovella Witherspoon. That's what I had named my baby before she died. Emma Andrews Witherspoon is on the birth and death certificates because at the time of my labor and her passing, I could not muster up the strength or the words to tell them a middle name. They simply used my maiden one. O.T. remembered the Emma part because I had told him in the eighteenth week my decision about what she would be called. He had forgotten about Lovella.

Emma was the name of my sister, who died when I was seven. She was younger than me by almost three years. So what I recall of her is mostly baby and toddler stuff. Crying, resting at my mother's breast, pulling on things—the table or sofa, my legs—as she learned to walk. I know that she was weak, prone to coughs and colds, a thready breath, Grandma Whitebead called it as she held the baby over a pot of steaming herbs, worry spread across her face.

Emma was lethargic, not very playful; she mostly stayed in the house, near my mother's lap. But I do remember one time not long before she died when I carried her to the creek and helped her climb a tree. It was the happiest I ever saw her. I lifted her while she grabbed for the sturdiest limb, and she pulled herself up until she was standing six or seven feet above me.

Of course I got in trouble for taking her outside without dressing her in hat and coat, for letting her get so high; but even my mother's anger quickly subsided when she saw the glee and excitement on her younger daughter's face and listened as she talked about what she saw from so lofty a perch.

That's the way I think of her even now, a little girl standing in a saucer magnolia tree, tiny cups of purple and white all around her, the sounds of her laughter, a thin voice calling out to the birds and butterflies that floated so near. I like the thought of her that way, happy and playful, surrounded by the sights and smells of spring.

After the death of my baby, however, I wondered if I had cursed her in some way, naming her after another child, a little girl, who had died unnecessarily. I considered the possibility that my sister Emma had returned and claimed her for herself since she had been disallowed most of the pleasures of living. I even thought it was fair. But that only lasted a few days. Grief doesn't let anything stay true for long.

Lovella was the name of my elementary school teacher. Dr. Lovella Hughes. She was black as coal, wiry, and not the least bit interested in excuses as to why you couldn't be or do the thing she knew you could.

It was, of course, in the 1930s, so the minority children were not permitted to attend the white school or be taught by white personnel. Dr. Lovella Hughes was the only teacher willing to travel up into the caverns of the Great Smoky Mountains and find and educate the children that no one else even acknowledged were living up there. She was hired by the state to teach the black children and the Cherokees.

The white teacher and the white school were in Bryson City, twelve miles away; and being half white and shaded more like my father's side of the family, I could have passed. But since my daddy was blind, literally and figuratively, he saw no reason for me to travel so far away just to go to a white school when I could walk down my driveway and across the field to the little cabin on the reservation where Dr. Hughes taught all nine grades. That's as high as you went in that school if you were even able to get that far. Most of the students were finished with the education system and Dr. Hughes's enormous amount of homework by the time they were ten.

She was hard, like wood, steady eyes and unyielding; and she would say to me, "Jean Andrews, there isn't a reason written down or spoken why you can't leave this mountain, go to college, and be anything you want to be. You have a gift, young lady, and God knows all about it. You just call him up and ask him what it is he's got in mind for you."

"Just call him up," she'd say, like he had a phone number and a direct line.

She thought I had a natural inclination for words and theorizing, suggested I considered journalism or science research. When I came home and told my parents what she had said, my mother smiled and nodded, her way of showing me she was proud. My father mulled it over much like a theological proposition and said, "Words and writing is a dangerous way to make a living; I'd pick the science option."

I laughed at the irony of this statement coming from a blind man trying to farm on the side of a hill. But then he continued. "I never want to see no record of the stupid things I ever said. Be like a snake you only hit and stunned, he'll be back to bite." Then he reached out his hand, a sign to my mother, who came over to his side, bringing him a cup of coffee.

Even though I understood my daddy's wisdom and had seen only one newspaper in my whole life, I still liked the idea of writing. I thought that with my teacher's guidance and support I could leave the mountains and the farming and make a life for myself with words.

But Dr. Lovella Hughes, the only person in my life who made me think I could do something other than dig up bloodroot or ginseng, milk cows, and grow a productive garden, left the mountain just as I was finishing seventh grade. She developed tuberculosis after caring for the Crainshaw baby when the mother died and the father just ran off. Everybody knew the baby was sick, that it had taken in its mother's bad milk; but Dr. Hughes was not about to let the child die just because he had a bad start. She cared for him as long as she could then turned him over to the state.

We heard that she lived a long time in one of those sanitariums near her hometown of Wilson and that she was never sorry for doing what she did. The baby grew up to become a famous lawyer, a senator or judge or something. To this day I don't think he has any idea how shaky his beginnings were and how one black woman, who rode a train, two buses, and a farm truck up the mountain to teach the children, gave him back his life.

When Dr. Hughes left I lost the motivation to keep learning, the drive to write reports or stories. So I quit school and helped on the farm and took care of my parents. There was always something that needed to be done, cows to be milked, weeds to be pulled, floors to be swept. And with just the three of us trying to make a go at harvesting crops and managing a farm, there was no extra time for studying or planning for the future.

Sometimes I think about how my life might have been different if I had finished high school and made it to college. I think I could have been smart and ambitious. I could have put the words together describing a life or researched the patterns of animal behavior. I could have been more interesting. But just like Dr. Hughes made a choice to put herself at risk to nurture the life of an orphan boy, I sacrificed the thoughts of being educated and clever and lived my life at home.

We stayed up there together, the three of us, working, figuring, managing, until I turned fifteen and Mama died from a heart attack. It was her third, the first two having come over a period of four years, leaving her weak-spirited and unable to walk a row of beans or stand at the stove and cook. After her passing, Daddy lasted just a few months. His trouble, though diagnosed by doctors as the same reason for death as Mama's, cardiac arrest, was of another sort. He simply quit living. Bleeding heart, the old folks called it. My daddy died from having been forsaken. He always thought he should go first.

After my daddy's death, I was briefly cared for by my father's family, his sister and her husband. But every day I would walk the three miles to our old house and stay longer and longer, until one evening I just didn't leave. I preferred the silence and the reminders of being a part of something to a house full of noise and routine in which I did not fit.

Aunt Carolyn would bring me food, check on me from time to time; but I found living by myself was not too unlike the couple of months I had lived with my daddy after Mama died. The only thing that was different was that the sunlight coming through the window seemed to last longer and the general spirit of the house, at least for a little while, was lighter.

For about nine months I lived by myself like a hermit. I wore my mother's clothes, the dresses, all made from cotton, a lavender one with faded blue flowers, a spring pink one dotted with tiny white buttons, a long black skirt that fell well below my ankles. I wore the pearl earrings she had won in a raffle and kept her silver combs in my hair. I donned her red blouse with beads on the cuffs, and I walked about the farm and even inside the house in my father's old work boots, the brown ones scuffed and resoled.

I lit candles and talked to the walls and the spaces in the air, like my family, even my dead siblings, was still there. I brought out the old high chair and set it near the table. I bottled milk and made juice. I cooked the way Mama had with spices of cayenne and mint. I baked bread and dried fruits so that the kitchen felt the same as it always did, hot and fragrant. I spoke to her while I kneaded and worked the dough. I asked questions. I sang lullabies. I called them to myself.

I took to smoking a pipe like Daddy so that the smell of tobacco, sweet and mild, remained along the edges of windowsills and high in the air above my head. I read stories from his favorite books, and I told him news of the mountain. I rocked in his chair, and I would not let him rest.

Once I realized that I was responsible for my dead family coming back, that I had asked for the spirits of those who had passed, it was too late because I had made it too easy for them to return and stay. It was all too familiar. I had created a house that was full and prankish, and eventually the dead ones were filling up the rooms and crowding me out.

I met O.T. when I left the ghost house and went into town one Saturday to sell apples and the herbs I had harvested. He was there with his family sightseeing, vis-

46

iting the mountains and the Indian reservation. It was late summer, August or September, the afternoons still hot, the sky heavy. He kept coming over to my table, tapping the fruit, rolling them across his fingers, smelling the ginseng, like he knew what he was doing.

He was handsome, attentive, a tall young man who claimed he wanted to be a soldier. He had dark brown hair and the bluest eyes I had ever seen. He was wearing work pants, denim, that were clean and unfaded. I think they were new.

He had on a tan shirt that was bordered in a bold black thread, a design of embroidered curls, that edged along the collar. He looked as fancy as a girl; and later I asked him why he was so dressed up. He announced that he was expecting to find me, that he woke up that morning and knew his future wife was waiting for him on that day. So he took a bath and shaved and put on his nicest clothes. And when he saw me, he said, he was certain that I was the one.

I was not nearly so convinced that we were meant to be together. It didn't seem to matter about how much faith I had, however, because before I or his mama and daddy knew it, he was driving almost up to the Tennessee border once a month just to visit me, the one they called "that dark mountain girl who both farmed and lived all by herself."

O.T. was easy to talk to in the early months we were together; he was shy and ham-fisted. He made me laugh. He made me feel pretty. He showed off a lot, more than he needed to, since truth be told, I'd have left the mountain with anybody.

It wasn't that I hated being alone up there or that things were too hard for me, a teenage orphan. It's just that once the house started growing my family's spirits, it became unruly. They had no regard for me or my space. It was as if they thought that since I was by myself and I had made things so satisfactory for them, I wouldn't mind the company of four unequal ghosts.

There were little things at first, hardly noticeable— dishes falling off the shelves, windows being pushed open, fires being blown out. But after a while they just got too comfortable staying there with me. It unsettled me.

Not that there were ghosts. Everybody in the mountains knows about ghosts. I expected ghosts; I lived on their property, hemmed in by the reality of death. It wasn't their presence that bothered me; I had asked for that. But rather what became upsetting is that they didn't respect me enough to believe I would mind their recklessness, their destructiveness. That they kept hanging around like they were sure I would keep taking care of them, cleaning up after them, staying awake for them.

I mean, what did they think, that I would stay up there for the rest of my life entertaining them? Fixing them suppers and pallets of color for them to lie in? Keep pasting and gluing together the things they broke?

It's true that I didn't have much and that I had longed for them to be with me. But I knew I was quickly reaching my limit and that I would have to make a choice to leave them to the place they wanted or die in resolution to join them.

So I closed up the house without saying good-bye, left the ghosts to fend for themselves, and took off with a young man called by two letters rather than a proper name. He brought me to his home in Forsyth County, married me, then promptly left to fight in the Second World War. I lived with his family, trying hard not to miss the one I'd abandoned, trying hard to make myself at home, away from the mountain, away from everything familiar.

I compensated for all that was missing by working hard. Since I preferred to be outside, I worked with O.T.'s brother, Jolly, and his father. I helped bring in soybeans, corn, and hay. I slaughtered cows, slopped pigs, plowed the fields, and put up tobacco.

Even though his parents did not like it much when he brought his new bride in to live with them, by the time O.T. had left and come home, I was more of an asset to them than a son. I was there. I farmed the land and helped raise the youngest child, Dick. And even though his mother always seemed to be studying me like she thought I brought in trouble, I know I kept that family farm afloat.

When O.T. returned, I had become grown and old like him. He was aged by the atrocity of war and by things he would never say out loud, and I by the costs of leaving home and being left alone too many times.

I see now that it was not the best way to begin my life as an adult, as a married woman; but I played with the cards I got. I know I gave the Witherspoon family the best of who I was. I worked hard. I caused no conflict. I did as I was told. But even though I left home and was

49

miles away from the mountains of my childhood and years away from the influence of an elementary grade teacher, I never forgot where I came from and what I had learned.

My family was bonded together, across life and across death. We shared a past. We had a common story. Dr. Lovella Hughes made me think I was capable of greatness. And even though my sister died young and greatness never came about for me, because of them I am a stronger, better person. So I wanted my baby to have that too, the bond of family, the possibility of greatness.

Emma Lovella. I gave her the name of more than just a sister, more than just a teacher and mentor. I gave her the name of a force. In the end it didn't matter; but when I was big and full of plans, it meant the world.

Emma Lovella Witherspoon, that's the name I chose for my baby because that is a name with history and hope. It is a name of promise. And for my daughter, when I was planning her life and calling her by name, when I was dreaming my dreams for her, giving her a path to follow, helping her begin, it was everything I could want.

5

I was awake and up at exactly the moment the snow fell. The TV weather forecasters in North Carolina give reports all night when a winter storm is passing through. And when they're right and precipitation really does fall, they follow it as it makes its way across the state.

"Notice on the satellite radar how the snow is falling

over Tennessee and making its way east. It should be here in the form of sleet or freezing rain in about four hours." Then they'll show pictures of a storm from last year and interview the transportation crews to find out which roads they clear first. Next half hour, it's the same thing.

They track it like it's a hungry beast walking toward us, threatening us, bearing down upon us. They make it seem that if we know exactly when it makes its way down our driveway and along our streets, we'll be safer and more sound than if we were met by surprise. "The snow should fall in the southern piedmont in thirty-seven minutes." No thief coming in the night here. The television stations will make sure of that.

I was not out of bed timing the storm. I just happened still to be awake and decided to open the blinds on the front window and check outside. It was 11:51 p.m.

Even in the dark I could see the heaviness of the clouds. The squeeze and grasp of the atmosphere to hold its breath. The burden of the weight. Clutching, clenching, gripping, it fought to keep itself together. Then finally in the time it takes only to blink one's eyes, only to be caught off guard, a quick jerk of your head, the clouds burst at the seams and there came a violent release. A bounty of white flecks shaken from the ripped belly of the sky.

Snowstorms in the mountains, when I was a little girl, were as frequent in the winter as the visits of mice in the storeroom. We expected the ground cover from November to March, sometimes April, to be crunchy and white. And because this is what I was accustomed to, I never thought much about it. Winter was white and brisk and stark. It was just the season, like dogwood flowers and daffodils in the spring, june bugs and squash blooms in the summer, rich golden leaves and dark green moss in the fall.

Now that I have been away from the mountains and their winters for so long, I am as surprised at the changes in the landscape when a storm rolls through as are the kids who grew up at the beach.

I never considered the splendor or the shield of the mountains until I left them. And the first five years I was married and away I did not sleep an entire night. I didn't understand for the longest time why I was restless. But then I realized that I felt exposed, uncovered. I would get up and check all the locks on windows and doors even though O.T. said they had never had a theft or break-in as long as he was alive. I couldn't help it because I felt bare without the presence of the hills around me. Unprotected and loosed in a way that kept me off center. I missed the boundaries of the Smokies, the edge of the peaks, the mounds of earth that separated me from whatever might bring harm. That's what I grew up thinking was on the other side.

I remembered, of course, all the things my mother had told me. I knew the stories of families hiding in the caves, fighting mountain lions and bears for food, the smallpox and pellagra and pneumonia that haunted the bands of displaced Indians trying to find a resting place for their ancestors' spirits, a home for themselves. I knew about the rampages and the thefts and the burnings.

I knew then and I know now that evil festered even within the protected place. That Shelly Threehawks was raped by the white deputies. That Lapis Gulley beat his wife and children, leaving marks on them that could not be denied. That the preacher lied to obtain land for his own house and farm. And that when my father was a boy he was forced to ride and break a horse that everyone knew was not meant to be kept. He was thrown then, knocked in the head, and made blind. That the Cherokee watered the evergreens with their tears.

But in spite of all that I knew then, all that I defined as truth, I grew up believing that evil was what happened beyond the green and sturdy summit. That bad things could not find their way across the rocky elevation. I believed that the hills were a fortress defending goodness and that what you did not name could never be called into existence.

Even today, more than fifty years since my leaving, snow reminds me of the mountains, which remind me of my childhood, which reminds me of the false but deeply regarded notion I held that harm and turpitude lie on the other side of what I cannot see. For a very long time I lived with that magical way of thinking and convinced myself that as long as I did not bear witness to betrayal or malice or vice, then I could pretend it would never reach me. As long as I never came face-to-face with trouble, it would not find me. And as long as I hid from the things that hurt me, I could hide from hurt.

I realize now, however, more than half a century beyond those sheltering mountains, that the most damaging belief that I brought with me from the years I lived in the shadow of the hills was thinking that as long as I did not lay open my heart and uncover the grief that collected there, as long as I did not share it, pour it out and bathe in it, as long as it was never discussed, it would not disturb the heart of anyone else. If it remained concealed, I believed, my sorrow could not harm the one I loved. It was a false belief.

I did not make it to Sunhaven the following day because of the weather. I called the nurses' station but the phones were not working. I could not stay connected long enough to have someone go to O.T.'s room and see if the woman was there.

The next day the roads were still icy so I had to wait another day before I could go. By then it was too late. Karen had asked the woman too many questions and scared her off. When I arrived early that third morning she appeared to be staying away.

If O.T. knew about her and missed her, he never let on. He never called out for her or spoke of her sudden disappearance. He did not seem distressed or anxious. It wasn't long after the storm, however, that his condition worsened and he became mostly unresponsive. They reinserted the feeding tube and moved him to the floor where higher-need patients resided. The top floor, the last stop on the way to heaven, one of the nursing assistants had said on the phone to a friend when she thought no one else could hear her.

I knew by the slowing of his breath, the blank stare from deep within his eyes, the unwillingness to participate in even the smallest gestures of life, that he would not last until spring. Having lived with my father after my mother passed, I knew all too well the decision one makes to die. And just as I could not alter the events of our past, I could not change what he was deciding to do.

There was no hill to hide behind. Death was marching toward us like clouds of snow being pushed across the horizon. And I would not take his choice away.

6

I think about Emma and wonder whether she chose not to be born. If she had a prophetic moment there in the warm dark pool inside my womb, envisioning herself in my arms, as my child, that she decided, seeing what she saw, knowing what she knew, that it was not what she wanted to do. Or if she was still in the hands of some other world that called her back because she was not ready or because she was too ready or that something was wrong with me.

"Failure to thrive" is how they define it when a baby, a born baby, chooses not to seek nourishment. It is not an uncommon experience. And I sometimes wonder if Emma just failed to thrive a little sooner than the others. I wonder if it was only some undetected pregnancy disorder or if my baby decided not to be mine.

"Fetal demise" is what they called it. That's the medical terminology, what was written on my chart. That's the name the experts give the experience of a baby born dead. And I guess that definition makes it easier for the doctors and nurses to deal with paperwork and the tedious cavities in their own hearts. I never asked who came up with such a term, only what it meant when I signed the forms to be released.

"It means your baby died," the young woman said, her eyes down and studying the words on the clipboard instead of focusing on me.

"Oh," I replied, remembering the word *demise* was also used in a court case Mr. Witherspoon was involved in after his father passed. It had meant that part of the farm had been transferred by lease. "Or maybe she was just loaned out for a while," I added.

The discharge nurse glanced up then and awkwardly handed me my copy.

I knew that she was dead when I woke up that morning. And even though there were no specific details that I could tell the doctor over the phone when I called with my concern, I knew it. It could only be described as feeling like part of myself had drifted away.

Certainly, there were physical changes. My breathing was different. My appetite had lessened. The lower back pain and the heartburn were gone. But mostly there was just the sense that something, somebody apart from me who was still of me and who, for more than half a year, had been living off what I took in, what I ate and drank and touched, surviving off my blood and my body, existing off my hopes, my breath, my will to live, that this somebody had now gone and had left me to myself.

I knew without ever having an exam or medical verification that Emma and the perpetual state of motherhood were no more. And though I was still as round and full as I had been just a few hours before when she kicked me so hard my knees buckled under me and I fell on a kitchen chair, I was now empty of life, void inside.

I left home without O.T. and drove myself to the hospital. I should have waited for him to return from Raleigh; he asked me to. I could have stayed and received some comfort from the other person affected by this loss. I could have shared that long bitter moment of disappointment; but I didn't. I walked out of the house, the bed made, the dishes washed, my overnight bag packed, the morning sun bright and promising, and drove to Mercy Hospital completely and undoubtedly alone.

I remember that a light frost had spread across the tops of trees, along the fields of forgotten gardens. I remember faces, people walking on the side of the road, waving hello and good-bye to one another, children riding on bicycles, to school, I suppose. And I remember how it seemed as if everyone standing or moving along the street where I drove noticed me as I headed toward town, a pregnant woman with a dead child.

I worried that if I lingered too long at an intersection or turned my head to acknowledge the curious stares, I would create some mass display of pity, some unnecessary situation of being assisted. So I drove in pretense that nothing was out of sorts. That everything I was doing—driving myself to the hospital, my belly too big to fit beneath the steering wheel, bearing the knowledge that my unborn baby was dead, choosing to make this journey by myself—was normal. I drove ahead, death frozen beneath my ribs, as if everything was as it should have been.

Once I got to the hospital and began to consider what would happen next, I assumed there would be an operation. I just figured they'd put me to sleep and take her out, cut me like she was twisted or I was too small, a cesarean section. Go to sleep eight and a half months pregnant, wake up sliced and childless. I mean, I wasn't the most clear I had ever been, but I do remember thinking, It's over, it is at least over.

But it wasn't. It wasn't close to being over.

How does a mother describe what it is like passing death through her body? How could I, in a lifetime or beyond, ever tell somebody else what it is like to stretch and tear and shatter inside just to let that which is already dead out into the air and expectation of life? How can a woman string the words together to let another know how it feels to do what is natural in a state of unnaturalness? To bring forth one's dead child and then to keep on living?

I have learned from my marriage to a combat soldier damaged in war that there are things that cannot be spoken. Things so terrible they cannot be named. And on my own battlefield I cried and begged and prayed for mercy—to die, to be wrong, to be delivered of all of myself, dead and dying. But I labored on without relief. Nurses stayed near but would not touch me, as if this death coming from inside me was contagious; I might infect their own mother dreams.

A doctor stood between my legs, the mind of a technician, the heart of a man who will never know. And I went from trying to keep her inside me to trying to get her out; and it seemed as if I were being split, broken, and pulled in two. Finally, when the doctor could no longer bear the wailing and the screaming, the agony of one more unproductive hour, he reached inside me with his clean and uncompromising hands and took her from me. Then he walked away, he and the nurses and my baby, leaving me opened and alone, having given birth to the only part of myself that I truly loved.

The next day I got up from the bed, my clothes neatly packed in my suitcase, a few papers in my hand, a blanket carelessly wrapped around me, and drove myself home.

7

I was in the house packing when O.T. walked in and thought somebody had broken in and robbed us. After rushing from Raleigh to be there during the delivery and staying with me through most of the night, he had left my room the next morning to go to the farm to cut a sow loose that had gotten tangled in a barbed-wire fence. He thought I would stay at the hospital until supper time anyway; but since I had driven myself there in the first place, stone-eyed and cool, again I would choose not to wait. I knew I could get myself home.

Even with the disapproving glances of the staff, a hasty phone call to the doctor, the whisper from an orderly to a custodian, an attempt to seat me in a wheelchair, I walked up the hall, down the stairs, and out the front door. Just as if nothing had happened. Just like I had gone to the hospital only to visit a friend.

When O.T. came in and saw what I was doing, he did

not have a word to say. I still imagine that it was the best thing he ever did in our entire marriage. He left me to myself, a self that at that point and for a long time afterward was not enough to share.

He only stared as I took my belongings and placed them in the car. He did not try to stop me or even ask what I was doing or where I was going. He sat and watched, eyes so full of anguish and despair I asked him to turn away. He dropped his face in his hands but did not cry. I finished packing and then walked away, leaving him there with nothing, just as the hospital staff had left me in the delivery room without any measure of sympathy or hope. I drove out the driveway and onto the street without even speaking a good-bye. I never considered his pain.

I wanted children more than anything; and when O.T. returned from having fought in Europe, closed up like an old wound, I staked my life and love more completely on this possibility than on the notion of creating a joyful marriage. I think I believed that having a child of my own would diminish my mother's sadness, which I had inherited from her, make it less noticeable, let her finally die and pull herself and all of the ghosts away from me.

I thought that a child would deliver us from the unrelenting silence we had managed since O.T. had come home from the war. And I suppose the desire to nest and give birth kept me from lifting the veils that, over many years, I had carefully and purposely draped across my own heart.

O.T., honorably discharged, never spoke of what he

had experienced during his time as a soldier. He never mentioned the places he had seen or the men with whom he lived; but just like I was forever scarred by the death of our baby, I knew he struggled with his demons. Late at night he would often leave our bed and I would find him outside, crouched near a tree or pacing behind the barn. I would call to him to come inside; and he would just move farther away, as if my voice was a command to march out into the fields.

Only occasionally would he mention his service in the armed forces, and when he did, the story was brief, the facts sketchy. Over a meal with his family he would casually comment about the chill of a European winter or how hunger can change a man. But if his brothers or friends wanted more details, he'd just switch to a different topic, his voice having grown distant and somber.

Unlike his family, I never asked what happened to him, how the battle years broke him, what he could not forget. I never offered him a place to release his burdens, slide open his heart. Since I remained closed regarding my own sorrow and grief, I never pushed my husband to talk about his.

O.T. did not seem to mind or be jealous of my obsession to have a child. Perhaps he too thought a baby could ease our disappointments. He accepted my desire without argument or recognition, right along with the house I wanted and built and the cool veneer that existed between me and his mother.

I think I loved O.T. even though I realize it was not passionately or with desperation. We were comfortable together, satisfied. And both of us knew, whether it was early in our marriage or much later, that we had what we had. In the beginning it was his mother who made sure of that. In the end it was simply our own method of measurement. We were what we had decided we were.

Mrs. Witherspoon headed off what she considered to be trouble when she noticed what was happening between me and Jolly while O.T. was away. She was subtle at first, only making sure we stayed busy and tired, that I would come in from the field and then have to babysit Dick or wash dishes. She made us focus on whatever crisis she discovered or invented; but then she took a fast and hard turn.

I never knew what she said to her son late one night, only that their voices were raised and sharp like arrows about to fall; but I soon understood after the community picnic and by the look on her face when she saw us walking up from the creek, clothes wet, feet bare, that she would not let things progress any further than they already had. The next day she was gone to town early, and she brought home with her Sally Pretlowe, the woman Jolly married three months later.

We were not naive or insensitive like she implied with her narrow glances and hypocritical prayers of confession that she prayed at the supper table. We knew nothing would come of what we were beginning to feel. We were both loyal to his brother and my husband and to the United States of America's war efforts against Hitler in Europe and the Japanese in the Pacific Islands.

We stifled the attraction, kept our distance in the isolated fields, pretending what we had was merely a relationship between a brother and a sister. And every night while we lay alone in our beds in rooms across the hall from each other, listening to the sounds of each other's sleep, not tasting, not touching, not stepping over the lines, I willed it to be so.

I guess I was drawn to Jolly because he was the same age as I when O.T. brought me from the mountains. He was a teenager, caught beneath the shadow of a strong and honorable oldest son and pushed from his mother's heart by a younger and more affectionate baby. He was solemn, spoke few words; and he reminded me of everyone I loved. There was nothing excessive about him. He lacked the confidence of O.T. and the tenderness of Dick. He was slow in everything he did, from math problems to fixing the engine of the tractor. He would disappear for hours at a time, down at the creek or out riding a horse.

He was awkward and yet easy to be with, unassuming and honest. And unlike O.T., who in the beginning seemed to regard me as some accomplished goal or some event he had planned, Jolly treated me like I was someone he could never have imagined. To my husband's younger brother, I was a complete and unexpected surprise.

Sally, the young woman Mrs. Witherspoon brought home for her middle son, was keen to both her mother-in-law's suspicions and her own intuitions about what was between me and Jolly. So that as soon as they were married and the war was over, she and Jolly moved to Alabama to work in her uncle's ladder factory.

I have only seen them four or five times in over fifty years, his parents' funerals and a wedding or two. I called when O.T. had a stroke. I thought it was the right thing to do. Sally answered the phone and was curt but appropriately sympathetic. She said that she would tell Jolly but that she wasn't sure they would be able to come. She suffered terribly with arthritis in her hip. "Had to have been all those years standing on a concrete floor," she added and then quickly mentioned a bridge game and said good-bye. Jolly never called; and I never made anything of it.

After O.T. returned from Europe and before Emma, I had forgotten what was between me and his younger brother. O.T. and I had to learn and relearn each other several times. He was burdened by a soldier's sorrow and I, because I so desperately wanted a child, by the disappointment of a monthly period. For most of our marriage, these experiences defined who we were. And even though I didn't really know him before the war— he came into my life and left so quickly—I knew that what happened during the years he was gone had changed O.T.

He was blank by the time he got home; and because I was already accustomed to the silent nights and the cooling of cravings, and then later when my baby came and went, we knew how to manage our life together. We expected little and were therefore rarely disappointed. Once I was off the mountain and living in the home of Oliver Thomas Witherspoon, his mother and father and two younger brothers, once I gave birth to death, I realized I hadn't a lot of hope for happiness.

I suppose it is this choice to accept an unfulfilled life that has caused me to be surprised that most people live their whole lives in a state of disappointment. I discovered this initially at the mill, where I spent the majority of my adult life. Loading needles and tacking elastic to the tops of women's panties, I was shocked to learn that most of the people there were expecting something more.

The women who gathered around the tables at lunch talked openly and without shame about the poor states of their children, the lack of opportunities for them in the textile industry, and the heaviness of unfulfilled dreams. Then they'd peer over at me, while I was eating my can of pork and beans or dry bologna sandwiches, and I'd just shrug my shoulders.

"No dreams," I'd say, remembering the hunched shoulders and empty palms of my mother's kin, the fading of the colors when Emma died. "Might lend itself to boring sleep, but it sure does let you get up in the morning."

And they'd stare at me like I had just grown pointed ears and a tail. Most of them did not know what it was like not to have dreams, least not the young ones, anyway. Of course, by the time most of them hit forty or so, divorced, bored with children who would not leave their houses, still working at the same job, they realized that they had not had a dream of their own in more than a decade. That's about the time the lunch conversations changed from lost hope to concrete plans for medical insurance and saved-up vacation days. Those were the conversations I deemed as sensible, and joined.

O.T. and I had planned to buy an RV and travel down to Florida, maybe up to Niagara Falls. But since I kept delaying my retirement because the boss would beg me to, by the time I was free O.T. started feeling nervous, having headaches. So that we never got to Bob's Vacations on Wheels, and we never camped in the Everglades. Soon Sunhaven collected most of our retirement money; and I didn't think much about our ideas for a long time.

In fact, before O.T.'s declining health and the sudden appearance of a woman named Lilly, I hadn't thought much about anything in a long time. Not the unrelenting spirits of my dead parents and siblings, who refused to leave the old house, or me and O.T. buying a Winnebago or the way Jolly would hold my hand, soft as rain, when he helped me down off the tractor.

Like the stories of a silent soldier and the way a woman's body cramps and tears during labor, some memories are simply put away deep, deep down and below, so that former things appear to have passed away and only those events at hand require attention.

Not since I was pregnant and then not, a mother and then only a wife, had I actually remembered things or felt things or noticed things, like the way a fly sings when it's caught in a spiderweb, the formidable strength of desire, and my father's empty eyes, which saw everything I did not.

I had spent so long turning away from life—refusing it, denying it, pinching and squeezing the sorrow and the pain and the possibilities—that the only emotion I could muster up when I finally met Lilly, other than the physical one of getting sick, was just the sense of being a little surprised.

Right before fainting, I saw a burst of color and heard my name being spoken. I said out loud, "Hmmm," like I had suddenly figured something out, nodded my head, and fell forward.

8

O.T. died on a Wednesday when the sing-along in the dining room down the hall from his room had just started and the nurses had all been called to a meeting downstairs. Since I knew for about a week that his time was close at hand, I had been staying all night, sleeping in the chair next to his bed, and showering in the bathroom down at the end of the hall.

The last days of his life I, not the nursing staff, bathed and shaved him, read him stories from the paper, and gave him things to smell. Oranges and strawberries, wet grass and lavender. O.T. had always noticed and enjoyed the smell of things, so I had Maude bring me stuff from the house or the barn or pick up something from the store that I thought might bring him pleasure. My perfume, a homemade brand that was a light floral scent he had found at some boutique in Chicago when he drove to a tractor show years ago, handfuls of dirt, tea with cinnamon sticks, and clove.

He enjoyed the aromas from outside the most, because when I held old tools or leather work gloves up to his nose, he seemed to soften and relax. I don't know if he really knew it or not, if it meant anything to him or nothing at all, I only hoped it eased his passing, helped him see that he was only going home.

When he did die I did not panic. I did not ring the call button on the railing of his bed. I sat beside him, having just placed a small sprig of lilac near his chin, rubbing his hand and listening to a cheerful pianist leading the group in "Bicycle Built for Two."

I smiled at the thought of passing to such a tune and wondered if the spirits who heard it would not come and take him until it was over, that they stood along the wall waiting, respectful, thinking it was some unknown tribal chant or worship song meant to send his soul into the next life.

He died without any meaningful final words or astounding moment of clarity like I have heard others speak of when they tell their dead one's story. Unlike even my mother, who died as she had lived, in sadness, or my father, who died begging for death to come, O.T. didn't suddenly turn to me and call out my name or tighten his grip or smile or shed a tear. He simply eased into it, accepted it, welcomed it like a man who had been waiting for his lover finally to come.

The warmth drained from his hand and the lines around his eyes and brow melted. His lips fell; and his breathing slowed and finally stopped. It was not desired or wrestled with, it was simply his time, and he acquiesced. Not a burden or an escape, it was merely death.

I clasped his hand tightly, pausing like the ancestors until the chorus was over; then I reached up and kissed him lightly on the cheek, straightened the sheets around him, and waited for someone to find us.

After almost half an hour, it was the housekeeper who came and bowed beside me, said a prayer delivering my husband into somebody else's hands, and quietly and quickly left us once again to be alone. Soon, once the news was told, a few of the nurses came, the administrator, and a chaplain; but none of them, just like O.T., had very much to say.

When I was asked by Mrs. Fredericks, the director of Sunhaven, about relatives to contact, I said politely and confidently that I would call his two brothers, Dick and Jolly, from home. She leaned toward me, placed her hand on my shoulder, and gave me a sympathetic squeeze. I returned to his room to wait for the funeral home personnel, and that's when a nursing assistant, one I had not known or noticed, tiptoed into the room and handed me a little piece of paper, torn from a notebook, with a name and number of someone, she said, who would want to know.

9

I met her in the parking lot while the hearse was pulling away. Sunhaven was more than an hour and a half from where she lived, but she arrived before I had finished filling out the forms and packing up O.T.'s things.

She got out of her car, crossed herself like I had seen the Catholics do, and walked in my direction, slowly and easily, like she was worried that she was moving too fast. But in only the second it took to see her approach, her gait, her frame, so clearly her father's child, I remember thinking, rationally and calmly, Everything now is different.

Just as she came near me, the wind whipping her scarf

69

from around her neck, a ribbon of pink flying past, my stomach knotted, my head spun, and I began to feel dizzy. I reached out to steady myself, searching for the railing that I thought was behind me or the bench I remembered being near the door; and she caught me just as I started to fall.

"Jean," she said and lowered me to the steps while I responded with a low and gentle hum.

A nurse hurried out and the two of them walked me to the family room. I drank sips of cola and kept a cool cloth across my brow. I ate a few crackers and said I wanted to go home. She stood near the door and watched.

The nursing home director put me in the passenger's side of her gold and white sedan and drove me to my house. I kept my eyes closed the entire way. It would be two days before I saw her again, before we finally spoke.

Lilly Maria Lucetti was born June 2, 1960, in Durham General Hospital, out in the hallway because she would not wait to come. She was a late spring baby. She is dark complexioned, olive-skinned, like a woman from Italy or France or somewhere on the Mediterranean.

She lived with her mother and her grandparents until she was ten. Then her mother, who never married, and Lilly moved out to a little house farther in the woods and just down the road from her parents. There was a lot of love and laughter, the days more sweet than sorry; and she considers her early years to have been serene.

She has large, oval eyes, like a delighted child; and she's as skinny as a teenager. She's held lots of jobs, predominantly public service positions; but she seems to feel most comfortable in a day care center where the children are allowed to play outside as long as they want and listen to music while they take their naps.

She finished high school in Chatham County, an average student, and completed two years at the university. Her educational possibilities were promising until she left when she was twenty to travel with a boy she thought would love her forever.

She met him in a park, both having planned to feed the birds and enjoy a late morning. They shared an egg sandwich she had brought and a six-pack of beer he had in his car.

He was bored with school, interested in what lay beyond, she said, with a roll of her eyes. So they left North Carolina and went west and west and west until they landed at the Pacific Ocean, saw the seals at Cliffside, and moved in with a friend who let them stay for free until they were able to find a place of their own.

Roger, the young man who swept her away from her studies, her home, and her common sense, left her in San Francisco, where the fog settles in like a family member and the streets are busy all the time. She was working in a shoe store then, persuading women that she could find them just the right shoe that could make their legs appear longer and their feet smaller. She liked the job only because she said that the tips of her fingers always smelled like leather and reminded her of the hides and skins her grandfather soaked and tanned in the barn behind their house.

She stayed there, satisfied, she said, by herself, living

in an apartment that was smaller than a closet, until she woke up one morning and couldn't remember the colors of fall or how a crocus bloomed in the snow, timid and yellow.

She missed the seasons, she said, the changes in the trees, the clarity at the edges of the sky, and the shapes of snowflakes. So she packed what she could and mailed it all to her mother's home, gave away the rest, sold her Yamaha scooter, and took a bus eastward to North Carolina.

Her mother met her at the Trailways station, eyes filled with tears. And Lilly's been in Durham working in retail or day care ever since she left California. Until now.

Her mother, she said, was glad to see her. Cleaned her room, redecorated it from something that belonged to a hippie adolescent to something that would be lived in by a young professional. She bought candles and picture frames and situated them nicely on the new Bassett light oak chest of drawers she bought at a furniture market showroom sale. She slept on a waterbed, and she often dreamed that she was sailing across distant but always calm seas.

Lilly said that her space in her mother's home was lovely, blue and mauve, like the feeling of dusk. She felt right about being there, welcomed, and unashamed for having left. And they lived together, mother and daughter, like roommates, like friends, for sixteen years. She left Durham only after her mother died.

When we finally talked, the day before O.T.'s service, sitting together in the parlor of Mackay's Funeral Home, she said that she left her hometown because she thought that Durham was just too full of death. Every road a reminder of a trip, an ordinary thoroughfare that calls up memories of her mother, the places where they traveled for groceries or dinner or just to get out of the house.

She said that even though she is beginning her middle-aged years, she might like to return to college, finish her degree, and teach. She claimed that she favors the thought of her own room in a long line of rooms at a school, her name on the door, and bulletin boards that she can change every few months to celebrate a new cycle of time.

When she told me of her plans, I thought they sounded fine, that it appeared to be a good thing for her to return to school, that it seemed like something that would make her happy. I didn't, however, comment on what she was telling me because in spite of the appearance of my goodwill, I was still trying to find a place in my mind where all of this could settle.

I was simply trying to figure out who we were to each other, whether or not it was even possible that I could accept her in the midst of such awkward and forced circumstances, whether simply knowing that she existed was already more information than I could handle.

When I did finally respond to all she had shared, all the reports she had given me, I asked her only how it was to have all of her family dead, to be without a mother and a father, thinking that this was something we had in common.

She was quiet for a moment and then answered, thoughtfully, decidedly.

"I have sat with so much grief," she said, "that I feel like I have acquired a new angle on life, that I have finally figured out the unprofessed secret that most folks never fully grasp." And here she paused again.

"Life happens in a moment," she pronounced as the funeral home personnel walked around us, trying to appear sympathetic and unobtrusive.

"Love is, at first, always a surprise, and the good things never last so they need to be savored." She continued as if she had been asked this before, as if she had already planned an answer.

"I understand now that life is quick and unpredictable, so that you need to pay attention to everything that happens because it is somehow intended to shape who you are."

I just listened as she went on to say that she believes in something beyond this existence, beyond this life, because otherwise, "our brief stays on earth," she said, as we sat in tall overstuffed chairs, "are such a flash on the screen of time that they would mean nothing."

Another family came in the front door. We both turned toward them.

"There must be another place," she added, "beyond this one, for all the dead souls to go."

I dropped my eyes away from the other grieving family members and faced the far wall.

She, of course, had not yet been told about my parents, the baby brother I never met, or my sister. She certainly had not heard the story of Emma. And as she talked on, so doubtlessly, about her thoughts and ideas of life and the hereafter, I wondered what she would do in a house where dead ones would not pass. I wondered if she could make them move on because she was convinced there was another world waiting for them or if she would stay awhile, living with them, like I did, until her own breath smelled of theirs. I almost asked how she could let love slip away so easily.

But I didn't ask such a question because I knew how it would sound. I knew that no matter how carefully I phrased it, no matter how I accented it with a touch on her arm or a slight, honest smile, it would come out spiteful and poisonous; it would seem like an attack.

And though I was certainly thrown off balance by her presence, dealing with this new knowledge of the betrayal of my husband, trying to sort through a death and now an unexpected life, I knew that she didn't deserve the consequences of all that I was feeling. None of this was her fault, her responsibility, or her doing.

We sat together in the funeral home near the body of a man whose life had touched both of ours, and I realized that she was not there to do me harm. She came to see my husband, her father, without the intention of ruining our marriage or causing trouble. I don't believe there was ever a single thought of malice in her head or in her heart.

She simply wanted to see the man her mother loved, tell him that he had never been forgotten, and show him how she was not abandoned or afraid. She thought she owed that to herself, to her mother, and to the father who never knew he had a daughter and who might just want to know.

In spite of how difficult it was taking in all of this

information, trying to let this young woman be a part of my husband's death, inviting her to speak freely of her life, I knew there was no way that she should be the target of my anger or disappointment. She, after all, had her own losses to suffer.

Lilly was not the reason for any of my grief or pain. She was only trying to discover her place, only trying to understand from where it was she came, only trying to find peace for herself.

I had nothing to gain from being rude or unwelcoming to O.T.'s daughter. She was not the cause for the break in my marriage. She bore no answers to my many questions. She was no different than I. We both were simply seeking solutions for the great mysteries of our lives.

10

Widow is such a lubberly label. Used like a medical condition or an exposition for unsavory behavior, it creates an illusion, a false image in people's minds that they suddenly think they know all about you. "Oh," they'll say, with just the right amount of familiarity and sympathy, "that explains everything."

At first it enraged me, then it merely irritated me, but now resolved, I simply use it to my full advantage. "I won't be able to get that library book back on time," I'll confess to the librarian, "because I'm a widow." And just like that I'm given an extension so that I can read the book at a speed I'm comfortable with.

"Won't be able to manage that volunteer food drive," I say sadly to the director of the soup kitchen. "You know," I say with just the right pause, "I'm widowed." And quickly I'm forgiven.

To the person at the bank I report, "Could you please handle all this paperwork for me?" Then I sigh and stare into space like somebody close to the edge. "I'm only recently widowed." And I don't have to worry about unwanted phone calls from collection agencies or investment personnel.

Maude says it's unfair and very unattractive for a person to use her weaknesses in this way. But I say, "Power to the people!" If they want to believe women are only as smart as they are married or that they lose their ability to create order or make decisions when their husbands die, then who am I to mess with a prevailing perception? Use it, I say, because life offers very few concessions.

It's been almost two years since I became the dominant figure in our marriage, since I first had to decide stuff for us, figure out things. Once the strokes started O.T. was no longer very clear or helpful. Dick and Beatrice helped some, but mostly I was on my own to take care of everything. On paper and involving the matters of detail, legal and otherwise, I was organized and even prepared for his passing.

In my more compulsive and lonesome moments when O.T. became institutionalized, I had taken the notion to get things ready. Power of attorney, safe deposit box, deeds, insurance payments—everything had been arranged and clarified. So that when he did die, there was so little to do I actually found myself bored. And especially with all the permission grief gave me to be slow and unproductive, I found that I had too much time to reflect upon the past and too much opportunity to think about the future.

Perhaps that's one of the reasons I was open to this young woman who had only recently made my acquaintance. Perhaps, because I enjoyed the luxury of an uncluttered mind, hours without tasks to complete, I was able to think about the possibility of letting her into my life. The other reasons, I suppose, had to do with common courtesy and understanding that she wasn't the one to be blamed, the desire to keep O.T. alive, and the hole that his death had left me with.

I think that if she had come at another time, appeared at a different place along my journey, I might not have made room for her, been as ready for her presence. But as soon as O.T. died, I realized that I was completely alone. I had no one to call family, no one to care for, no one to depend upon. Maybe I let her in because for the first time in such a very long time I was painfully unattached. I was lonesome; and I let her into my heart just because she arrived at the exact moment when the last one who took up space had gone.

There is no doubting the fact that she looks just like O.T. She has his narrow lips, the smooth Witherspoon brow, the stern chin. There is the loose way she stands that reminds me of his rangy, long, poised profile when he used to stop in the field and measure how far he had to go, eager and unassuming.

O.T., of course, was bigger, stronger than Lilly, but there was still a clumsiness about them both that made him and makes her easy to approach, comfortable to talk to. And it was more than just these physical attributes that they shared. There's a way about them, an air of comfortable familiarity like an old pair of shoes, that in the beginning made me want to be around her, keep her near, so that my good-bye to my husband didn't feel so final.

Maude said that there was discussion and even a vote at her church women's meeting about whether or not Lilly had the right to come into our lives. "It was six to five," she said, "that she should have stayed away." And then she added, "but you really can't count Marcella's vote since Janice Smith told her when to raise her hand, and because, after all," and here she cleared her throat, "she was only recently widowed."

She said this without even realizing that she was talking to another one of these women whose brain everyone assumed was now missing in action. After she said it I couldn't decide which part of Maude's stupid report made me the angriest. But I guess it was the part about making judgments about Lilly and what she did or did not have the right to do because this is the part I would not let go.

"And people wonder why I quit going to church." I said, hot and fast. "If that's all you women have to do on a Tuesday night during your so-called Bible study, then I suggest you examine the choices those in the group made." Then I was loaded and shooting.

"Why didn't you take a vote as to whether or not Masie Reece should have had breast reconstruction or just used a prosthesis? Or whether Carol Ingle should have bailed her son out of jail on the third time he was arrested? Or whether Linda Masterson made the right decision to raise her sister's child like she was her own? Maybe you should spend your time judging the choices you all have made rather than picking apart the lives of those you know nothing about."

She was backing out the door, but I drew her in. She had started it, and I was going to finish.

"Did you know your daddy?" I asked, already sure of the answer because her parents lived with her until they died. She had always been close to both her mother and her father. Say what you want about Maude, she was a dutiful daughter. She nodded.

"Did you know how he looked when you pleased him? What you did that made him laugh? Do you remember how he picked you up when you were a little girl and danced you around the kitchen table or helped you climb a tree? Do you recall how it was to be wrapped up in his arms, feeling so completely safe that you were not afraid of anything? Of anything?"

I was not to be stopped.

"Do you remember when you were angry how he teased you in just that silly way that made you forget why you were mad in the first place and the special name that he only had for you? Can you say, beyond a shadow of a doubt, because of all these things you alone have, things that are only yours, things that you pull out to cushion your withered heart that confirm for you what you had always suspected, that he loved you?"

I was a streak of anger.

"You answer me that, and then you tell me that a child doesn't have the right to find the man who's responsible for bringing her into this world! That she doesn't have the right at least to see his face, learn his voice, hear him say his daughter's name, her name. Because whether she does or doesn't isn't for anyone else to decide, anyone but her. She gets to make up her mind all by herself. All by herself," I repeated.

Maude was afraid of me, but that did not make me hush.

"And I strongly suggest that you and those nosy, backstabbing church ladies remember that the next time you carelessly raise your hands to vote on something you know nothing about. You remember that." And I walked out of my own house, leaving my neighbor alone to sort through what had just exploded before her eyes.

By the day of the funeral we were friends again, and in spite of all the screaming I did to Maude about her church cronies, they all showed up at the funeral. They were fidgety around me, careful with their words, and just a little too affable toward Lilly. They probably came more out of obligation or curiosity than concern, but I appreciated the effort and was kind to a fault. I think they all mean well and that their intentions are generally honorable. It's the meddling and the malicious appraisals rendered without thought that leave a bitter taste in my mouth.

The church is full of self-righteous people who love to claim grace for themselves and their families but who have a hard time doling it out to those who don't quite measure up.

O.T. was active in his church while he was growing

up, his mother took care of that. But after the war when he wasn't convinced that he still believed in God and couldn't sit without moving for more than ten minutes at a time, he went only for family weddings and necessary funerals, making sure he sat on the end and near the back.

Since I was used to going to church services in a tent, a living room, or out under the trees near a creek, when I got married and moved down from the mountain, I never found a church building in which I felt comfortable. So that when O.T. came home and made his religious change I was glad not to have to sit in a luxurious sanctuary pretending that the gold and the stained glass and the well-rehearsed choral music ordered things and helped me to pray.

If I worship anywhere, I go to the A.M.E. Zion Church just up the road and situated down a long driveway in a grove of trees. The music, like the people who attend, is soulful and ardent, the sermons fiery and made plain, and the love and the pleasure are without pretense or burden.

The pastor, the Reverend Vastine Yarborough, works full-time at a sheet metal plant an hour and a half away and is only at church the first Sunday of every month. The other three Sundays a deacon or an elder, a college student or Bible teacher, leads the service. I have found that with the humility of a lay leader fumbling with the words of Jesus and the soft, low hums of the elders helping him or her along, it feels the most like church to me I have ever known.

The message is always simple, informal, and to the

point that God is not partial to anyone. We must all, regardless of what we have or have not done, kneel at the throne of grace with only ourselves and the risen Christ, who stands ready to intercede. It is just simply a reminder to love, and I feel the same way there as I did with the church folks in the mountains. God is most impressed with us when we undo ourselves before him; and church happens when, without judgment, we allow others to do the same.

It was because of the ease and the acceptance I have received both before and since I have become a full member of the Sharpley Grove A.M.E. Zion Church that I decided to have O.T.'s funeral there. He went with me to worship only once, but it was the only time since the war that I have seen him sit still through an entire church meeting.

I watched him out of the corner of my eye for the entire two hours. He relaxed while he was there, sat in ease, the lines on his face softened. When we got home and were sitting at the table eating lunch, I asked him, "O.T., how did you like worship?"

He smiled. "It felt good to be with you there," he replied in his clear, simple way. And he reached over and touched me on my arm. "That's a good place," he added, giving me the clear indication that he approved of me being a part of that community. It was as if he understood why I joined, why I liked to attend.

Even with his guard slightly lowered at Sharpley Grove, however, he still only went with me that one time. And I never pushed for him to join me. I have always thought each person has to find his or her own way, chart their own path. I suppose in O.T.'s mind because God had not yet made clear to him personally the answers to the questions that rattled him and because there had been no undoing of the recollections he continued to clutch and could not let slip away, communal worship was not the place he sought comfort, church was not the safe harbor for him to dock.

He never spoke of his questions and memories with me, never let me know. He took them all with him to his grave and, I guess, on and beyond. I figure this because the gospel is clear that what is loosed here is loosed there and what is bound here will remain bound there. Even heaven cannot pry open the things we will not release ourselves.

The funeral was probably noisier than most of the other guests were used to, a little too long for O.T. But I'm quite sure that he wasn't there anyway; and I could have cared less what anybody else thought. I was pleased. There were flowers, but not so many that the church smelled like an artificial death. Words of sympathy and assurance were read by the trustees. Acknowledgments were given. Loretta Parker sang a solo. The men's choir rendered two songs, and Pastor Yarborough preached about the sacrifice of the soldier, the qualities of a good husband, and the ultimate price that Christ paid for all.

I think Lilly thought he was a bit too heavy with the Jesus talk, but I was satisfied. It felt just like what it was supposed to be, a service of celebration with a reminder that there is something bigger than us, something weightier than our own desires, our own heartaches. It was exactly what I needed, especially since I was now having to find ways to deal with O.T.'s infidelity and, further, the fact that he loved another woman more than he had loved me.

Dick and Beatrice were there, from Hope Springs. Jolly came, without Sally or any explanation of where she was or where he had been; and there were more than just a few well-wishers and old friends. The reunion was sweet. I'm sure everyone went home satisfied that O.T. had a nice send-off and that his widow was doing better than they imagined. I'm sure there was lots of talk about Lilly and who she was and how unbelievably strong I appeared in the midst of such strange circumstances. I must admit, I put on a very good face the entire two-day event.

But late that night, when the service was over and everyone went home and the house, having settled, was as quiet as a stone, I discovered that I was exhausted, tired down in my spine, up along the curve of my neck, and in my somersaulting mind. I felt yanked and pulled like a piece of old rubber. I drank some hot tea, tried to lie down and rest; but I was one long, raw, pulsing nerve. I had extended myself beyond the point of ease.

Saying good-bye is hard enough. Doing it at the same moment, with the same breath in which one is invited to share a greeting of hello, is simply more than a body can cope with. All the information, all the secrets, all that had been hidden, put away, kept from me, suddenly filled up my room, and there wasn't enough space to sleep. It was worse than being with the ghosts.

I wanted my husband back. I wanted him to have to

deal with what I was having to deal with by myself. I wanted him to explain what had happened, help me understand. I wanted to hear him say that what he had done was wrong and destructive and that he was sorry.

And then I wanted my heart to quit hurting, the muscles in my spine to settle, and there to be another body, his body, curved into mine as we lay in that quiet, moonlit room. I wanted to feel his arm pulled around my waist, his breath, warm, behind my neck because what I really wanted was not to be alone. Finally, truthfully, I wanted most not to be alone.

I waited, even hoped; but I was not visited from the other side. I was not attended to by angels. I received no spirit. I had nothing but doubts and questions and sorrow, and no one but myself with whom to lie.

I fell upon my bed and wept. Each tear, a thought of O.T., a memory, a moment from our life together, the unexpected things we were and were not to each other. I wept for Lilly, this woman who broke open so many closed and denied truths, this child of my husband. And in spite of how unlikely it sounds, I wept for a woman I never knew, the woman my husband loved.

For the truth is, I will never know if O.T. realized who Lilly was, why she appeared, and what her coming meant. I can never say whether or not he understood what was happening at the end of his life, if he knew how troubled I would be. But it was certain that before he died O.T. had thought of Lilly's mother. He did remember something that they had shared together. He did still hold a place for her in his heart.

At the time it happened, of course, I had thought

nothing of it. I had deemed it only one of his random and confused moments, an episode demonstrating a lack of clarity in his thinking. But I knew later, as I lay on my bed of grief, trying to make sense of it all, wrestling with what I did and didn't know, that it was, in fact, her name he called out the last day he was coherent.

Clara. Clara Elizabeth Lucetti.

Perhaps, I thought, just before I dropped into a deep but comfortless sleep, the wave of sadness having crested and fallen, if I know her, I can know him. And if I know him, maybe I can know myself.

11

The only child of a migrant farmer from Nicosia, Sicily, and his wife of sixty years, Clara Elizabeth Lucetti grew up and lived in love. In 1942 Vincent and Maria Lucetti and their thirteen-year-old daughter were stowaways on a boat sailing from Italy to Spain and then paid, using all the money that they had stolen or saved, to sail on a steamship headed to the port at New York City, in the United States of America.

Vincent was more than thirty, a foot soldier under Mussolini, when he fell out of company and walked three hundred and eighty-seven miles to his home after he witnessed the killing of more than a hundred Jews and was ordered to dig their graves.

Afterward, but not often, he would tell his wife how he pulled shut the eyelids of many of the victims, including a little boy who died beneath the bodies of his parents. Not killed quickly by the Italians' bullets, he had been only wounded by the gunfire and then smothered by the weight of his dead mother and father, who had twitched and then fallen on their only son. Vincent would tell the story he had heard and memorized from a tearful old woman who had seen the atrocity. He told it as he stroked his young daughter's hair. Easily he pulled his fingers through the dark locks while he silently imagined the painful last thought of a man tumbling after his dead wife and upon a child who would never know what it was to grow up.

There were other things he saw and could not forget; but only this story would be discussed. It was for him a moment by which he marked his life and measured his living. It was for him the reason he left his homeland, the reason he quit speaking the language, and the reason he supported violence when it was meant to fight against tyranny and genocide like what had occurred in World War II.

He never said so out loud, but quietly he hoped the father of the boy knew of his tenderness and saw how he shut the child's eyes while saying a prayer for their souls. He hoped the man was able to find some peace in having seen this insignificant but sincere act of mercy. It was not enough, he knew; but maybe for the father's spirit, he would see what Vincent had done and it would bring enough comfort for the man to turn and walk toward heaven. It was the hope of a parent's heart.

Because Vincent had great experience working in the vineyards, when he arrived in the States it didn't take long for him to make himself invaluable to the owner of a winery in New York; and for a while he seemed satisfied. After a couple of years, however, he found he could not take the bitter cold of the northeast winters or the long flat season without enough work to do. So he and his family, Maria, his wife, and Clara, their lovely teenage daughter, moved south first to Virginia and then to North Carolina. Vincent worked in tobacco and cucumbers, sweet potatoes, cotton, and any other field that did not freeze and harden by the first of November.

They found that they liked the mid-Atlantic region, the mild seasons and the starry open nights; and he soon made enough money to buy his own farm and sell vegetables to restaurants up and down the eastern seaboard.

He sold tomatoes, cherry and pear ones mostly, that were sweet enough for sauces and salads and strong enough for easy shipping. He almost cornered the market on spring onions because everyone knew his were delicate and tender, without too much of that customary sharp sour taste. He grew carrots and asparagus, did well with okra and squash; but he was mostly a tomato and onion man because the plants were easy to maintain and the climate and soil where he lived were just right for their growing.

It was said that by the time Mr. Lucetti sold his farmland and retired, he was one of the wealthiest men in eastern North Carolina. Lilly says they never wanted for much but that her grandfather sent a lot of the money home to his sisters and brothers in Sicily and never approved of a lavish lifestyle. He was hardworking and frugal, but he did not trust the banks or the government. So while he left a good nest egg for his wife and daughter, he had not taken care of necessary taxes and insurance.

Much of the couple's life savings, therefore, was soon tied up in overdue payments to the IRS and given to doctors and hospitals and ambulance drivers since his progressive and later terminal illness of lymphoma devastated the family for more than fifteen years. They learned the hard way about the health care system in America, how a rich man can quickly become poor dealing with cancer and the experimental treatments every oncologist wants to try and every insurance company refuses to fund.

He died sometime in the early 1990s, much like he sailed from Europe to America, rugged and worn, ready for anything and certain that he had already seen the worst. Maria stayed by his side, curled next to him in the bed, and his daughter and granddaughter slept on the floor at his feet. When he took his final breath it was said he lifted his head and faced the women whom he loved and said *"Mi vede,"* translated from Italian to mean, "He sees me," and then he closed his eyes and passed.

Like an obedient wife always just behind her spouse, Lilly's grandmother, Maria, died a few weeks later, her hand to her chest and a look on her face that made it clear that she had once again done as she was told and was able to carry out her duty as Vincent's partner. It was what made her happiest.

Together Lilly and Clara cleaned the house and sold it, finished paying the incurred debts, sorted and saved, and reminisced about the lives her grandparents had lived. It was bittersweet and nostalgic as Clara told story after story about their beginnings in this country as immigrants and the journey that had brought her this far. And so it had been on a clear Monday, the same day her mother was scheduled for her mammogram, the second in three weeks, that Lilly was finally told about her father, a farmer like her grandfather who was kind-hearted and doting but had a wife he would not leave.

12

At first I wanted to know, and both the desire and the story seemed harmless. After the funeral I convinced myself that hearing details might help me see things more clearly, sort through events, order the chaos. I believed that it would bring together the loose ends of my life, of my marriage, that it would tie the unstrung cords together again.

I thought that if I had some kind of an understanding of who Clara was and how she fell in love with my husband, it would answer all of the other questions of my life. I thought it would unburden me, free me. I had not considered the power of it, the memories it would unleash, or how much it could sting.

Lilly refused me in the beginning. When I asked her the day after the funeral to come and tell me about her mother's love, she said it was not hers to speak. She did not think it was something that I should hear or even something she had the right to tell since Clara herself had waited so long to share with her daughter the story of her lover.

I called again a week later. I told her that she was the only one who knew, the only one who bore some kind of witness to the contents of my husband's heart. I confessed to her that I needed to hear the story to balance out the grief. And reluctantly, four days later, she drove up from Durham, sat in my kitchen, and told me everything.

There were moments that I had to leave the room. I feigned the need to go to the bathroom or to fetch a tissue, but the truth is, I left to catch my breath. Hearing the story of my husband's infidelity, the news of a love I had not known, felt, at times, like a swift, hard blow to the ribs. But each time I went down I got up, shook off the hurt, and finished the ride. I heard it all, slowly and completely, until it no longer kicked, until I understood.

Clara met O.T., Ollie, when she was twenty-nine, almost thirty. He was almost ten years her senior, although the differences in how old they were never surfaced. He had aged from the war, but his heart seemed young enough that he could at least appear to have overcome the deep but critical scars.

They saw each other three, maybe four times before he ever had the courage to speak; and when he finally did, it was only "Good morning" and a comment about the color of her dress. It was pink, dusty rose really; and he had said it reminded him of the sun at dawn.

She blushed at the attention and the intimacy of what had passed between them. And even though it was ever so slight, unnoticed by anyone around them, unregistered, and insignificant, Clara and O.T. both recognized it, knew it, knew the magnitude of it, the possibilities of it, and the danger in it. Only one of them, however, understood fully the betrayal that took place the moment the relationship was merely considered.

Clara was the head waitress for the morning and lunch shifts at a small restaurant. She had never waited tables before; but she discovered that she liked serving food and making her own money, so she worked at the job for a number of years.

Shy, close to her parents, she had not made a lot of friends in high school. She was well liked and easy to be around; but her father was strict, and she had therefore missed out on most of the social activities for young people her age. At the restaurant she was no longer under her father's thumb; and she found she enjoyed the attention she received from her customers, mostly men, who liked the way she filled out her uniform and the effortless way she served them.

She worked as a server for eight years before she was promoted to manager. Clara was good with figures, reliable, smart in crisis situations, and got along well with all the other staff. The waitresses liked her because they knew she understood what the job entailed. And she took care of them, filling in for them if they were not able to make it to work, switching off the busiest and most profitable sections so that everyone got the chance to make a little money, and letting them take breaks when they needed them. The cooks liked her because she wasn't afraid to work in the kitchen alongside them.

All in all, Clara and the restaurant business were a perfect match. The owner valued her work highly, paid her well, and even allowed her the opportunity to buy him out on several occasions. She never would, however. She liked the arrangement as it was; and when the owner moved to Miami and the restaurant was sold, she was happy to go back to waiting tables, finishing her career just as she had started it.

Clara told Lilly that she was sure O.T. had noticed her on his first visit to the diner. Usually, he had told her, if he stopped in Durham on his way home from the tobacco sales or the state fair, he went to a hot dog place way off the highway in the rear of a gas station. He liked how they kept the buns steamed and soft and that the chili was homemade. The grill was quickly shut down, however, after a grease fire and the health department's immediate response.

It was Billy Barker who told him about the diner where Clara worked and the blue plate specials that were always hearty and never more than three dollars. Once he drove into the parking lot just off the interstate, had a bowl of the Italian wedding soup, and caught the eye of the woman who seemed to be doing everything, O.T. soon found himself needing to take more and more trips into the Raleigh-Durham area.

He stayed with Clara for two years before he broke it off because his wife, I, had lost our baby. Lilly stopped at this point, nervous that what had been said had upset me. I nodded to show her that I was okay, placed my hand across my rising chest to convince myself, and then she continued.

Clara spoke very little, Lilly said, about the two years she and O.T. shared. She told her daughter only that she had never before or since felt the passing moments of her life so deeply. She noticed things like the smell of flowering jasmine that draped along fences on her way to work, tiny yellow blooms that had been there for years but she had never seen. She heard sounds that people made, the hum of old songs while they worked, the heavy sigh when someone they loved walked away.

She noticed colors, soft subtle colors in the sky, along the lips of teacups, and in corners where tiny pieces of glass had been swept. She felt alive, she told Lilly, alive the way she thought we were born to live but that we rarely understood, alive and attentive, the way we are at those significant transitional moments, she told her daughter, the way we are when we're in love.

As Lilly recounted the story, I remembered the night during those two years that O.T. and I shared one rare event of intimacy. I remembered the night when I slipped aside the disappointment of all the years of infertility, all the years I had been barren, all the years we had tried and failed. I remembered, as Lilly ordered the history, the night that Emma was conceived.

When I was in my late twenties and the doctor reported to me that I was unable to bear children, that my ovaries were too small, too unproductive, I did not want to believe him. I spent many months the way I had spent more than ten years, filled with desperation, calculating my temperature, counting down days, and regulating intercourse, until eventually I grew exhausted. Ultimately, I gave up hope and gave up sex.

It had been more than a year since O.T. and I had been together; but on that night when our baby was created, I forced my husband to try again. I surprised him when

I begged him to lay with me; but I did so because my monthly cycle was just right for conception and because earlier in the evening I had dreamed of the coming of spring.

I saw the sky open and fire falling upon meadows, flowers blooming, dead trees filled up with life. Later I awoke with the sense that everything, for the very first time in my reproductive system, was right and ready. That my egg would not die.

That my body had somehow shifted and made room for another.

When O.T. came in from working I was crazed with desire, not because I wanted and now had my husband, not because I even wanted him to share in the depth of what I was feeling. I pleaded with him to have sex with me because I was finally and once again in the position of considering the possibility of motherhood.

I did not even notice the way he would not look at me. I did not pay attention to the obvious lack of kissing and tenderness. I did not even see that he was in love with and committed to a woman whose child, unlike mine, would live. I only wanted to have that baby. Once it was confirmed that I was pregnant, I would not have another sexual encounter with my husband again. After all, it was then no longer necessary.

When Emma died and I ran to the beach, O.T. made one last trip to Durham to tell the woman who had learned life's secret of love that he would have to be loyal to his wife. Because, he would tell her as she turned her head away so as not to show him her tears, it was his unfaithfulness, his bitter lies that had killed the baby I had wanted and that together we had chosen to deliver.

Clara would then decide not to tell him that she had missed her period for more than two months, that she was often queasy and fatigued in the morning, that she noticed a faint stirring within her belly, and that she had felt, a time several weeks before when they had made love, an unusual sensation that something more had happened. She did not in any way let on to her lover that she was pregnant with his child. The weight of his guilt was already so overwhelming she was sure the news would crush him forever.

Clara said good-bye to O.T., gently let him come and now go, without demand or claim or even an announcement that she was now left to raise a child alone.

As I heard the conclusion of Clara and O.T.'s love story, the end of the one she told her daughter, I understood that once he said good-bye, once he left the desire of his heart, my husband came back to the house I had started building while he was away at war, returning fully this time, completely.

Clara stayed on at the restaurant, never betraying the identity of her baby's father, never sharing the secret with an understanding waitress or a cook who would have married her and made the child his own. She never told a soul, never asked for assistance, and never seemed to need anyone.

Even her parents could not persuade her to confess her lover's name. And though they were angry at first, ashamed, they did not turn away from her, they did not put her out. She stayed with them, and they raised the child with her; and as Lilly says without needing to be believed, it was a peaceful and lovely life.

Lilly said that she came searching for O.T. only to see his face, only to see the other half of herself. Her mother had told her who he was simply because she thought her daughter had the right to know. She did not tell out of spite or bitterness or because she had now changed her mind and wanted to upset her former lover's life. She said that she had always expected their affair would not last, that he was much too much of a gentleman to leave his wife and that she had always respected his decision to go home.

She did not make her daughter promise that she wouldn't tell or that she wouldn't try and find him; she knew Lilly would have to make up her own mind about these matters. She only asked that Lilly remember and honor the love her mother had freely given, a love that bears and believes and endures.

It had been this love that had kept her from telling O.T. and forcing him to make a decision that was more painful and difficult than she could ever imagine. It had been this love that kept her silent and strong; and she only asked that her daughter hold this in her heart when she got ready to do something with the name she now knew. He was more than just her father. He was a husband, somebody else's husband, a man who had not known the consequences of his affair.

"Be careful with what you know and with what could hurt him," Clara would say before she died. "He was the man I loved."

And so Lilly had come, quietly and unobtrusively.

When she realized that O.T. was institutionalized, she thought she could come and go and not be discovered. She had not wanted to upset me, she said. And I smiled. For she had actually calmed me down.

She told him who she was, but he had not seemed to understand until she said her mother's name. When she said the word, *Clara,* he turned and faced her, his eyes filled with tears, and then he reached out and took his daughter's hand.

There, with his hand on top of hers, they cried together. And Lilly says she thinks he knew who she was. And she is satisfied that even though she had not felt as if any large or significant piece of her puzzled life had really ever been missing, she had kept a space, not filling it with anything or anybody else. And that when she finally met O.T. and told him who she was, the grasp of his hand, the tears in his eyes, all of whom they became in that whirling, unclouded moment had fit. Mercifully, my husband's daughter said with an unspoiled assurance, for her it had fit.

We sat in my kitchen on that cold winter day, the story spread out before us like pieces of clean laundry snapping on a line. And when my ribs finally quit hurting and I could breathe, I was suddenly reminded of a difficult period in my parents' marriage.

When I was thirteen, my father became convinced that my mother was leaving him. He was prophetic, of course, because it was only two years later that she died. But at the time of his premonitions, like Maude and her water dreams, he was not clear about the details, only that she was going to go. He believed that she would leave him for another man.

I remember it was the only time in my life that I ever saw him curse his blindness. Throughout all of my childhood he never acted worried or troubled because of his loss of sight. He never seemed disabled or handicapped because he always managed to do what he wanted to do. He was never to be pitied. But there, in those tortured few months as he grew more and more certain of my mother's betrayal, he clawed at the sockets of his eyes, praying that he would finally be able to see.

I would hear him late at night behind the house, crying and ranting at God for making him less of a man, making him unable to peer into the eyes of his wife. He would scream, "If I could see, then I would know that she was lying, know that she was in love with someone else! I could see it for myself!"

Mama heard him as well; and night after night she would go out and lie at his feet, begging him to believe her that she was not going away, begging him to come inside and lie with her in bed. I would watch from my window as she took his fingers and slid them across her brow, pulled them along the curve of her neck, then gently placed his hand inside her gown, to feel the beating of her heart, she would tell him.

"John," she would say in just the way only she could, "feel my heart. Feel my heart. It will tell you what your eyes cannot. It will tell you that I only have love for you. I will never leave you." She would cry to him, "I am yours for all time."

And they would fall into each other while he begged for mercy and assurance and she gave him all that she had. Then he would come in, ragged and afflicted, and she would love him back to life.

"Why does he do that?" I asked my mother after one of his dark nights. "Why does he think you are leaving him for someone else?"

"He loves me too much," she replied as she began fixing his breakfast. "He knows no other way." And she turned to me, pulling me into her arms, and then sent me out to school, burdened and pleased at the same time.

I realized on that morning, sitting at the table with Lilly, that when a nonattentive wife reflects on her marital history with a new line of information, specifically that her husband was having an affair, things begin to make sense that never did before. The late-night arrivals or early-morning departures that he said had to do with traffic, the new shirt or pressed trousers that he claimed he needed, and the way his eyes could move past the matters at hand and out across a horizon he never explained.

I understand that O.T. and Clara cannot be the cause for every failed conversation or unloving moment we had between us for the two or so years they were together, but it certainly does clear up a lot of things I could never completely grasp. Like why he looked at me as if he owed me something or how, for the longest time, he never seemed comfortable being near me. I realize that the years he was with Clara, he was restive and uneasy, never fully attuned to the things that happened at home.

Nothing he did, however, led me to ask him about his behavior. I was never troubled or worried enough that I said, "We need to talk," or, "What's going on with you?" Unlike my father, who begged for proof of my mother's fidelity because he was so madly in love with her, I went on with my marriage without hesitation or pause even when I knew O.T. was not engaged.

For so many years of our life together, I focused my energy on things beyond ourselves. I was distracted and unavailable. I concentrated so completely on getting pregnant, staying pregnant, pushing away the sorrow, I never saw that my husband was preoccupied or guilty.

Suddenly, hearing the story of my husband's affair, I realized that it's possible that if my father loved my mother too much, I did not love O.T. enough. I'm not saying that I excuse what he did. My husband broke his vow to me; he was not faithful. He did not tell the truth. He loved another woman. I was betrayed.

But the truth is, I could not stay angry at him for very long. After all, even though I did not sleep with someone else, didn't I commit the same offense as O.T.?

Even years after Jolly was gone with his new wife, I continued to give great and weighty consideration to the idea that I had married the wrong Witherspoon. After all, isn't the gospel clear? The lust that we hold in our hearts makes us just as guilty as the lust that binds two people in bed.

The truth is, O.T. and I were more roommates than husband and wife. We shared responsibilities around the house, took our meals together, had a few common interests.

In the beginning, he stayed with me because he felt responsible for bringing me into his family and I stayed loyal to him because I was the wife of a soldier, because my husband was a brave and honorable man. Years later, we stayed together simply because of inertia. Grief and guilt can sometimes fall like a thick, smothering blanket. It can cover a lot of desire.

I wanted a family more than I wanted a husband. For too many years I was more devoted to the idea of being a mother than to the actuality of being a wife. And when we were together, it was making a baby, never making love.

While I was absorbed in becoming a mother, O.T. left me to myself. He knew better than to step between a woman and her longings, and so he found himself tempted and drawn to the dreams of another. Dreams that were completely and all about him.

I cannot blame him for finding what I was not willing or prepared to give. I am only sorry I did not know before now. Perhaps I could have given him my blessing since he had found what I had not, pleasure in commitment, happiness multiplied and divided with someone other than a ghost.

I buried my husband, gave him to the earth; and I did so with thoughts of forgiveness. And I hope that he has found himself in a place where it is kindly given. I hope that in those final days when he did meet Lilly, before the time of his death, he was relieved of his guilt about Clara and Emma and me.

I pray that as he entered into that new realm he was welcomed and received, redeemed and sanctified. I pray that every unwashed, unholy strand of his being was made clean.

I hope that before he passed, Lilly came into his life and unbound him, that just as the coming together fit for her, it fit for him too. And that in death and in heaven O.T. has found mercy and release. Because even knowing what I know, hearing what I heard, even with the punch and stupor of realizing that he loved someone more than he loved me, I pray that maybe and finally, O.T., my husband, can rest.

13

In my rented room at the beach, where I stayed after Emma died, I cut out pictures of children and taped them to the mirror, all along the wall, and near the headboard of my bed. I began buying children's clothes, girls' mostly, pink and white and yellow suits that I could bundle over the smooth newborn body that I imagined would appear if I prayed hard enough. I purchased a pacifier and diapers and tiny slippers that were meant to be worn to church. All these things I smuggled quietly into the motel, placed them around me, and waited for my dead baby, for Emma, to arrive.

I had spent Thanksgiving at the Holiday Inn eating the lunch buffet with a few travelers, a bitter waitress, and a busboy who did not speak English. I was not sad or in need of pity, I merely thought a full meal might shift a bit of my sorrow. It was one of only a few times I ate out during my retreat from life. Most of the time I just had crackers or cereal or soup I fixed on a little camping stove the innkeeper let me use in the office.

I found that just as when I was fifteen and orphaned,

I was perfectly capable of being alone. It seemed as if I needed no one living to be near me, only the ghosts of those who had left. I cleaned the other guest rooms to make a little money and cover the expenses of my rent. I read magazines and cut and dyed my hair. I slept until eight and went to bed at ten. I rarely spoke a word. But in spite of my silence and hair that was too blond for my dark eyebrows, I appeared to the people who watched me as if I were perfectly fine, as if the callused pumping organ that used to be my heart was still in normal working order. To anyone who noticed, it seemed like there was nothing out of sorts. I, of course, knew otherwise.

In my room, between the walls, the front window, and the floor, the clamor of despair was trying to snatch the life from the weak fingers of a woman who had lost herself. I welcomed the slow but confident march of resignation and even begged for it to take over my severe and tortured thoughts.

I did not realize what I was doing at first. It was without thought, unplanned. I would simply see a little dress or a soft pastel blanket, and I would add them to the other items I had gone to the store to buy. I never said a word, never asked about a size or answered any question about how old was my baby. I just began collecting things between Thanksgiving and Christmas to give to the child I knew would eventually join me.

It took a few weeks, but I soon saw signs of my own departure, recognized my actions established during the bereavement of my parents' deaths. I noticed how I began counting and setting aside my dollars and quarters, saving for a particular piece of clothing or toy, stuffed bunny or storybook. It was familiar, like choosing to wear the dress my mother most loved, the hat that bore my father's prints.

I saw the break when I started having to sneak out of my room so as to keep the other guests from peeking in and seeing the shrine I was building. It was exactly the same as before, when I had not allowed Aunt Carolyn in the house, taking her casseroles from her and obstructing her line of vision when she would come over to see about her peculiar, grieving niece.

I started feeling desperate and unhinged the way I did when Daddy's pipe went out and the cold touch of the tobacco signaled that something was gone. When I ran out of my mother's perfume.

I remembered that I had once before chosen to make my life with death and that Grandmother Whitebead had been the first ghost to come to me with a warning, a heavy strip of tar left on the frame of the door, a sign that what I chose would leave me fastened, stuck between two worlds, gummed and tied for the rest of my life. I had not listened to her then; and only after the spirits became heavy and selfish did I begin to search for a way out.

This time, when I saw the bloody stain in my pants, I felt a faint but definite pull to recognize and at least acknowledge that I was once again making the subtle but obvious choice to live with who and what had already passed. That I was giving way for the dead to swallow me whole.

For a few days I fought it. I was feverish and loosed.

And then I started to smell the fragrance of pine and coal, the odor that lingered inside my father's house when everyone was gone but me. I tried to air out the room, get rid of the smell; but it only grew stronger and more ponderous. I was creating that which I wanted to come.

So when I could no longer stand the stench that thickened in my mind, I fled my room like a stranger had invaded it. I ran down to the water, begging to be baptized, praying to be relieved. I hadn't even realized that it was on the eve of Christmas. So that just as most families were beginning to open presents and sing carols, when church bells were ringing in the birth of the Christ child and friends gathered to enjoy the holiday, I took to the ocean, the flood of tears, knelt then lay there beside the slippery hand that seemed, after time, to push and pull me back to life. I, in a fit of despair, delivered myself to be given and returned.

The whole night of Christmas Eve of the year of my baby's death, I stayed at the shore. Hour after hour I remained in the palm of my pain, unable to move away. Until finally, when I could cry no more and the sea had reached further into herself and I had not drowned, I dragged myself from the sand and the broken shells, returned to my room, fell into the bed, and slept three days. When I awoke, I packed up only what I had brought with me, left the baby gifts as they were, and drove home. I left the mountain once again.

There is an old Russian fable that tells the story of village women who lost their children. Out on the edge of the community was a small shed where the mothers, still fresh from their grief, were allowed to stay for six weeks. Food was brought to them by the other women; and except for the knock on the door signaling the arrival of a meal, there was no outside contact.

At the end of the appointed time, the women from the village set the small cottage on fire. It would be up to the woman inside, the mother who had buried her child, whether she came out or stayed inside and perished. If she could not face her past and future, so intricately tied to her feelings of that particularly clear morning, then she gave herself to the flames. If she found that she desired to fight the smoke and look for some reason to live, she came out of the burning shed and was given her first responsibility in her new life: to rebuild the sorrow house for the next mother who would need to go and choose.

There by the ocean, on a frigid Christmas Eve, I had laid myself down, brought it all up, and laid it down. So that when the flames began to singe, the smoke of hell like a crooked finger motioning me to join death, I stood up and walked out of the burning house and returned to what had been mine.

I came home from the beach, the holidays over, and found that there was still a little artificial Christmas tree in our living room. I noticed its flashing lights, red and blue and orange, a small display of cheer and hospitality, when I turned off Highway 301 and onto Old County Road, the street on which we lived.

When I left the ocean, I made the choice to live, to return to O.T., to be once again his wife, a seamstress at the mill, a friend. I left the sorrow and the dreams and the smell of charred sticky wood there at the edge of the shore, a heap of kindle and ash; and I never returned to pick it up.

I let it go out, simmer and cool, and finally die. And since O.T. and I never discussed it, I believed any embers of hope or disappointment or shame had long ago subsided and been put out.

I never considered that O.T. had kept a small fire burning.

14

Almost a month after the funeral, Lilly came to Forsyth County to help me go through O.T.'s things. I thought there might be something that she would want, a pair of cufflinks, a book, his watch, maybe the service medals that I thought he kept locked in a jewelry box in a safe out in the shed. Since I had not known her very long and wasn't certain about her sentimentalities or her pleasures, I wasn't sure what thing or things she might choose to help her remember my husband and her father.

I thought she might like the picture of him when he was young, an old but undamaged photograph just before he entered the war. It was my favorite; but I thought maybe she would want it. He stood tall and proud, his shoulders square and his hands tight but open at his side. He wasn't grinning or toothy; but he had a smile of confidence that seemed to dictate his posture and his readiness. He was dashing then, brave and eager; and Jolly had captured his brother's strength in the moment he clicked the shutter. I thought it spoke well of who he had been.

Perhaps, I thought, she would prefer having his military records or the trophies he had won at the state fair for his treasured bulls, the Black Baldies. I thought she might want his father's pocket watch or an old sweater, something personal and cherished, something, anything, she could keep like I have kept my grandmother's china, to remember how I belonged. I thought she would need something to balance out the heavy force of her mother's side of the family.

But I was wrong about her, what she needed, what she thought she had to have. It turns out, she didn't want anything. Said it seemed too artificial, made O.T. into something he had never been to her. That she understood he was the world to her mother, but he had merely been handed down to her. And besides, what she knew about him had been so late and sketchy, there wasn't anything, other than the memory of the moment when she says he realized who she was, that she believed she would find that could capture what it was she had not yet started to feel.

She had not come searching for him to uncover anything about her life but rather only to add to what was already there. Then even though she would not take anything of his, she offered to help me just the same since she knew how endless and painful the process of sorting through death could be.

Lilly is smart that way, clear about things that I have to sit with for a while before I figure them out. I am not nearly so lucid. Things never feel so plain. And I found that I am drawn to that quality she possesses, envious of that strong sense of herself. And I wondered as she gently but without any attachment handled the belongings of her father, how things might have been different for me if, at a younger age, I could have had that same idea about myself.

We went through his chest of drawers and desk, the sparse side of his closet and the shelves in the garage. Not many of his things were left since I had boxed up and given away a lot when he went to Sunhaven. It didn't really take so long in the house. And after we finished we had a bite of lunch. When she asked if that was all, I remembered that I hadn't ever gone through the shed where he kept his tools and farm equipment.

I had not yet decided what to do with all his work things. And I hadn't seen what was in the safe wedged in a corner. I had always had all the necessary papers, wills and insurance contracts, kept in a safe deposit box at the bank, so I hadn't really had a reason to go out and open it. I hadn't really wanted to open it. It was and always had been the collection of his private matters, his sanctuary, his altar. Before he died, and even after, it felt obtrusive and somehow disrespectful to go there. But knowing that I would have to get into that shed and the safe sometime, and since his daughter was there for support, so open and willing, I decided to finish what had been started and straighten up the rest of his affairs.

"It smells like my granddaddy's barn," Lilly said as we walked into the old structure.

I smiled at her and watched as she reached up and touched the tools and the reins draped alongside a saddle.

"O.T. loved to farm; and he loved farm stuff." I glanced around at all the rakes and shovels, saws and hammers. "Maybe Dick wants it all, or maybe I should just have an auction, let someone else take care of all this."

"Mama and I did that. We went to Savannah because we didn't want to watch people handling all Papa's things. Thought it would be a nice getaway. See a new city, bum around. So that's what we did. When we got home, there was nothing left but a check from the auction house and a yellow sticker on the last lawnmower with a sign that read Sold."

Lilly sighed, remembering, I guess, and stuck her face into the leather. Then she walked around the tractor, away from the door, where there was a light hanging from the ceiling. She switched it on.

I stood with my cheek against the fender on the rear wheel of the tractor. It was cool, and I closed my eyes, remembering how it was to see him driving away in the fields, knowing at the time that the entire day would pass before I saw him again.

Lilly was at the back of the shed where the safe was placed, low beneath the workbench.

"You know how to get in this?" She fiddled with the tumble.

I walked to where she was. "Seventeen, nine, thirty-seven."

She faced me, surprised that I would remember a set of numbers I claimed I had never used.

"He kept it written down in a lot of places. I learned it," I said, "like a phone number."

She shrugged and waited for me to bend down beside her. She was expecting that I would choose to unlock it.

"Go ahead," I told her. And I rested on the front tire.

It took her a couple of times to get it, but finally it clicked and the door pulled open. It was too dark to see inside the safe, so she reached in and took out his jewelry box, which I knew was there, and a fistful of papers. She handed them all to me while she felt around, making certain there wasn't anything left. When she was sure she had gotten everything she shut the door and turned to see what we had found.

At first glance there wasn't anything surprising or unexpected. His army discharge papers, an old farm deed that didn't mean anything anymore, pictures from the war I had already seen, the soldiers gathered and friendly, and a few documents that his father had given him about his genealogy, the Witherspoon family tree.

The jewelry box was locked, but a small key was taped to the bottom. I pulled it off and unlocked it. Lilly sat down on the ground in front of where I was seated, and I placed the box on the tractor beside me and opened it.

His military awards were inside, his mother's pearl ring he had brought to her from France, a faded old hair ribbon that I was sure wasn't mine, a sketch of me he had penciled when he drove up to see me before we got married, and a folded piece of paper stuck way behind everything else in a small compartment, under a narrow and secure lid.

I held each of his army medals, the ring, the ribbon, and the folded paper, then passed them on to Lilly, one at a time. I steadied the picture across my lap, keeping it for myself.

Lilly handled the items I gave her, examined them, delicately placing them beside her as she went from one to the other. When I handed her the ribbon, she rolled it in her fingers, held it to her nose, and closed her eyes.

Without either of us saying it out loud, we knew whose it was. We both knew it was Clara's, the only thing O.T. had kept, the only thing to remember her, the only thing that linked him to Lilly and her to me. She stretched it out and then tied it in her hair. Quickly, I turned so as not to watch her.

I can't say if it was embarrassment, shame, or even disappointment to find proof of my husband's love for someone else, to see a token, a tangible expression, a keepsake of something he fell into and then forsook. To find and hold a thing, a memory, that he had kept and hidden and treasured even when it was all over. I do not know the motivation behind the action, only that I turned and looked away. I fumbled with the picture in my hands.

"It's Mama's," she said after a few minutes.

I kept my eyes down. "Yes, I imagine it is."

"Does it hurt you that he kept this?" Her voice was as innocent as a child's.

"A little," I confessed. I finally glanced up. Her hair was pulled back, away from her face, and I saw again the resemblance to O.T.

"I can understand that," she said.

A flock of geese flew above the shed heading toward the pond behind the field where we used to grow tobacco. They were loud and clamorous, sounding like a room full of angry old women. We smiled at each other. The cries faded and a silence fell.

"He picked you, you know."

I turned away.

"I mean, you can say it was because your baby died or because he was a dutiful man or because he was racked with guilt; but regardless of why, he still picked you."

I glanced down at the picture my husband had drawn of me more than fifty years ago, a picture he drew when we were younger than Lilly, when we were filled with hopes and grand ideas, when we were not old from life. I studied the lines, the curves, and remembered the day he had come to the mountains with his pad of paper and pencils, how he had coaxed me into going out behind the house to sit under a tree. I remembered how he worked so long and diligently, trying to capture in his drawing, he said, the likeness of my deep beauty. I remembered how I blushed when he said that, because no one had ever called me beautiful. No one had ever looked at me so completely.

"Yes," I answered his daughter and remembered the moment of tenderness there in a yellow meadow, framed in wildflowers and a wide blue sky. I remembered that in fact he had made it very clear, on that day and others that were to stretch before us, that he had chosen me—to draw, to love, to marry. And somehow the memory and the reminder of his choice eased the awkwardness that had pushed its way between Lilly and me.

After a few minutes she reached up and touched me

on the arm. "What about the paper?" she asked, changing the subject.

I handed it to her without opening it for myself. I thought it might be something else that was more hers than mine.

She unfolded it and began to read. "I don't know what it is," she replied and handed it to me.

I took it from her and realized that it was a deed to a cemetery plot on the far side of town, a park that I had once told O.T. I thought was genuinely lovely in spite of the fact it was full of death.

"I'm not sure," I said. "It appears as if he bought a place at Memorial Gardens." I tried to see the date of purchase. "I don't understand that," I added, "since we both have plots with his parents." Then I had a flashing thought that maybe I had buried him in the wrong place.

"Do you know where it is? Maybe we should go see," Lilly said, and she waited a minute then got up from her seat and began walking toward the front of the shed.

She was so confident and so easy about it that I agreed. I took a last glance around at the old place where my husband had spent most of his life, switched off the light, and followed her. I dropped off the jewelry box, the drawing, and safe papers in the house, found a jacket since it was cold outside, and got my purse and keys.

The sun was high and bright as we drove almost to the county line. It took about fifteen minutes to get there, and neither of us said much. A comment about the coming of spring, the way she loved to ride in the country, a reminder to myself to take the car to the station. I drove as if I was only going to the store or to vote. It didn't seem at all like what it really was, that I was riding out with his illegitimate daughter to see what else my husband had hidden from me for almost forty years.

The green land sloped toward a pond where ducks were always lounging about. There were a few trees, the flowering kind, dogwood and Japanese maple, and a bridge that seemed to signal a passageway from one life to the next. It was restful there, I had told O.T., a good place to go and remember a life. I parked near the entrance and turned off the engine.

Lilly got out of the car first. And suddenly as I sat watching I became afraid. I remembered the things I had said about the cemetery, the way he seemed to take note, and in just the amount of time that it takes to recognize the face of a friend, I knew what I would find.

I sat there for what seemed a long time before she tapped on the window, right beside me, and motioned me to get out of the car.

"What's the matter, Jean?" she asked as I opened the door.

"I think I know who's here," I said, still not moving from the driver's seat.

"Yeah?" She glanced out across the cemetery, the green and rolling hill marked with flowers and stones, telling the stories of those buried there. "Family?" she asked.

I nodded. Then there was a long pause.

"You want me to go find the plot and come back to tell you?" She waited for me to answer, and I remembered how quiet O.T. had gotten when I called and told him what I feared. The baby was dead.

I shook my head. "No, I'll need to go."

She turned away from me and waited until I felt a little more steady and stepped out of the car. I pulled the deed out of my purse and handed it to her. "I don't know how you follow this," I said as she unfolded the paper and began to read over it.

"It says row 44, plot H." She studied the cemetery. "But I don't know how you figure out what is row 44. I don't see any numbers." She shielded her eyes as she inspected the graves ahead of us.

As I focused out beyond the paved circle where we were parked, I knew without counting. It was simple once I saw the tree. There next to the mountain ash on the far side of the hill, where the grass was deep green and the angle of the sky seemed to lift the ground right into the rays of the sun, that's where I knew she'd be.

Mountain ash, like friendship and old grief, offers something unique and different with each passing season. There is a pattern to it, an order that becomes familiar and yet unpredictable, both warm and glaring, at exactly the same time.

In the late spring it yields great clusters of milky white flowers. In summer it is full and fernlike, providing restful shade. In the fall, when the other trees turn and fade, the leaves of the mountain ash stay red and yellow and the branches drip with red berries, supplying birds with food. In winter, while other trees are barren and unwelcoming, the berries remain, a resource that is dependable and abundant.

European mountain ash is the most widespread of this

variety in the United States. For more than a century it has been rooted and maintained across North America. It was one of Thomas Jefferson's favorite trees, evidenced by the large numbers of them planted in his garden at Monticello; and it was my grandmother's favorite tree. Near the reservation, we were surrounded by them.

The old folks called the tree witchwood because it was said that the burning of the bark and limbs could be used to exorcise witches or rid a place of spirits. When Mama and Daddy died, an uncle from my mother's side left a small stack of twigs outside the front door for me to burn and send away my family's ghosts. But I knew what the sticks were, and I didn't light them.

My grandmother used to pick the berries and make tea that we drank for an upset stomach and to prevent colds in the winter. I loved the mountain ash; and O.T. knew it. That was, after all, the tree in his picture. Of course he would have planted one near the grave of our daughter. Of course he would have kept it strong and healthy. Of course he would have taken care of my baby's resting place.

I pointed out to Lilly where she was, and slowly we walked together. I felt the weight of the sun on my neck, the pull of my heart to return to the car, and the silence of my new stepdaughter as together we marched up the hill to a place I had long pretended did not exist.

I do not know what I thought they did with Emma's body. I guess I figured they just destroyed it in some way, burned it or threw it out. I thought if they called it fetal demise, they just ridded themselves of it in some orderly fashion as if it were only a diseased organ or amputated limb.

I never considered the idea that O.T. would have made arrangements with the hospital staff, with a funeral home, and with a cemetery to care for our dead baby. I never thought he would have done such a thing, tender and careful. I just did not expect he could have known.

I stopped for a second before we got to the grave, to gather myself, I suppose. I felt a wave of fear, a rush or dread; and I reached out my hand to hold Lilly's. She took it, and together we walked the last few yards.

It was a small heavy stone, chipped, old but sturdy, with a statue of an angel sitting on top and an etching of a small flower in each corner. "Emma Lovella Witherspoon," it read. "Born and Died November 11, 1959. Loved and adored by both Mother and Father."

I touched the marker, drawing my finger inside each groove and line that spelled out my daughter's name. I felt the angel, the tiny petals of the flowers, the rough edge at the top, the smooth corners at the bottom. I dropped to my knees and felt the earth, cold and unyielding, that had buried and held my child.

I stayed that way for a while, kneeling at the grave, just as I had at the ocean when I decided to let her go. Lilly remained there behind me. She didn't shift from side to side, clear her throat, or even reach for me. She just stood there, quiet and undemanding, letting me have the silence and the sun for as long as I needed it. When I finally felt ready, I got up, walked over to the mountain ash, pinched off a small limb, and laid it at the foot of the grave.

I stood back as if the prayer of benediction had been said, marking it as time to go, turned, and walked to the car. Lilly waited and then followed. And as she came striding toward me, the perfect reincarnation of my husband, I shook my head, realizing how my entire life had been weighted and balanced by death.

15

"What's it like being pregnant?" a young girl at the mill asked me as she watched me stop in the middle of my sewing and rub my stomach.

She was no more than sixteen, somebody's daughter sent into town to make a little money for her family living on the farm. The mill was full of girls like her, who never left home but were sent away, learning now about life from conversations with older, wiser women, discovering the world from the inside of a too-hot-in-summer, too-cold-in-winter warehouse where we made and boxed fancy underwear for rich ladies who could afford the finest in lingerie.

All the mill women dreamed of how it must be to wear fancy underwear, to have stacks of such lacy, silky things lining our drawers. We sewed while we fantasized about the good life, the life we had accepted would never be ours.

We wore the rejects, the mistakes that were left in a large bin near the lunchroom for anyone to go through and find what they could. We took them home and fixed them, knowing that to use company time to work on the irregulars was grounds for being fired. We took them home, satisfied that we had all that we needed, grateful that even though we made luxurious things we'd never wear, at least we had a job, at least we were off the farm and managing things for ourselves.

Wanda, the young girl who asked me about being pregnant, was not a good worker. She was slow to learn the machines, always late with her work, more interested in the women around her than in meeting her quota or filling the boxes. She was forever away from her machine, standing behind someone else, asking something about how the rest of us lived.

"Doesn't feel too good right now," I answered her, trying to rub away the low ache of skin stretching farther and tighter than it was meant to go. "My back hurts; my feet are so swelled I can't wear any shoes but slippers. There's indigestion and this high-strung baby kicking me in the ribs." I poured out a long breath. "And I'm so tired I feel like, if she'd just lay quiet with me, I could sleep all day and all night long."

I leaned over and stuffed the completed batch of underwear I had finished into the empty carton at my side.

Wanda came closer to me, peeked around to make sure no one was listening to her; and then she whispered, like what she was saying was too dangerous to be spoken out loud. "My sister said it was like being God."

She stopped. Her eyes darted from left to right. "But you ain't supposed to say that," she added, shaking her head. "My mama hear somebody say something like that, and she'd fly after them with a broom."

"Why?" I asked, noticing the time on the clock. I was getting hungry and hoping it was time for dinner.

"Sacrilege," she answered. "Can't nobody claim to feel like God." Her voice was clipped, sullen, a child in confession.

She waited. "You feel like God?" she asked.

I shrugged my shoulders and pulled out another stack of unfinished panties. "I don't know," I said.

I thought about what she was asking. "I feel like I'm part of something like a miracle, something that pulls every part of me into it—my spirit, my blood, my dreams. That the pieces of who I am are being drawn into this life growing inside me. That I'm being multiplied and divided into somebody else."

Then I stopped what I was doing and considered God at the beginning of the world. I thought about how it might have been, the loneliness at first, the powerless echo of one single voice, the desire to share what was imagined and dreamed, the appetite and ache of a heavenly heart.

I wondered if creation started with an inkling, a feeling, that eventually developed into a choice that God made. The choice of pulling God's own self into winding rivers and flashing stars and small glossy leaves.

I thought about the notion of color, a wish for magenta and sapphire blue, pale pink and deep, deep brown. And how God then breathed out marigolds and black-eyed Susans and plush green carpets of rye grass, the exploding laughter of God's beaming yellow sun. Rich black plums, tiny red berries, and ripe golden peaches. Trees and flowers and long, curled, white blooming vines.

I imagined that at first there was an idea and then there was a reality, a hope and then the unfolding, a "why not?" and then a "yes," all streaming from the fingers and eyes and marrow of God.

The spinning planets, the emerald seas, the wide, wide spread of purple fields and long lovely meadows. All of earth and sky and watery depths, all of light and darkness and life. Mountain and sand, valley and stream, marbled stone and ice-capped peaks, all from the dancing and delighted bones of God.

Then, in the gathering of the colors, the whirling moons and stars and planets, God looked around at all this creation, all this space filled with possibility, bounty, and without limits; and God desired, for creatures, beings like Godself to roam and honor and celebrate the world carved from the Creator's own imagination. So God gave birth.

Like a woman pushing and groaning and delivering of herself, God gave birth. A flood of water breaking forth into creeping, crawling life. God gave birth to lions and beetles and pelicans and mice. To sleek graceful horses and soaring fearless eagles. To amoebae and insects and frogs and worms and snakes and fish. God brought forth them all, in joy, in zealous expectation. God brought forth them all, out from God's own great and mysterious and fertile womb.

And when the world was round and brimming with all the animals of the one host, alive and thankful, exploring and explored, God still thought that there was need of one creature more.

God decided, God chose: "Just one more image of myself." And there in the final hour of creating, expectant and full of faith, God knelt upon the newborn earth and breathed a deep and hopeful and lusty breath; and out from the great womb we came, male and female, separate and same, marching, calling and called; out of the hope and heart and soul and dream of God, we came. Children, infants of heaven, we came.

I turned to the young teenage girl who asked what this inexplicable gift to me was like, and I took her hand and let her feel the baby rumbling inside my belly.

Her eyes were big as plates as she felt the life stirring within me; and she smiled and pulled her hand away.

"My sister was right, miss." She nodded her head and stepped away from me as if I had made magic. "It's just like being God."

And I laughed and went back to work, at ease and at one with myself and my full, leaping womb, divine.

16

"Do you think I shouldn't have come?" Lilly was dipping out the ice cream to put on the apple pie I had made for our afternoon together.

Maude turned toward me, distressed. She pulled at her blouse, pushed her hair behind her ears, her face a bright shade of red. "Oh my, I think I left the stove on at the house." She got up and headed out the door before I could say anything to convince her it was all right for her to stay.

The door slammed behind her.

"What was that about?" Lilly stuck the spoon in her mouth, pulling it out slowly.

"You know Maude." I took a bite of my pie. "Crazy as a bat."

The apples were tart, Granny Smiths, not like the ones from around home, not like the mountain apples.

"Well, what do you think?" She stared at me with those familiar eyes.

"Does it matter what I think?" I pushed a napkin toward her plate, wondering why she asked me such a question.

"I'm not sure it did when I came, but now I'm curious. What do you think of me showing up just before your husband died?"

I put down my fork and I paused. I thought how Emma would be almost Lilly's age. How she and I might have sat together at the table like this, talking about her father, the neighbor, or what I think about something, eating pie too close to dinner time. How she might have been similar to Lilly, similar to me.

I enjoy having Lilly come by these days. It's usually only once every couple of weeks. It's never strained, feels like she belongs, relaxed and comfortable. She's thinking about going to the university nearby, so she drops by after she's had an interview or a tour or taken a look at apartments in the area.

She spent the night once, slept in the guest room. And I liked it. I like having her call and drop by. I like our conversations about the mountains and restaurants, gardens and children, the thought of even going to Italy together.

I'm sure lots of people consider the fact that I have a relationship, a meaningful relationship, with the daughter of my husband and his lover as pathological, that I was in need of finding my dead daughter and that she was searching for her missing father, her recently deceased mother, that we're both sick and desperate for a fix. But it doesn't feel that way, doesn't seem to be clinging or unnatural. And since no one can really know or understand all the layers of another person's life, why would I care what anybody else thinks anyway?

It was only difficult, strange, in the beginning when she called, when I heard she was visiting O.T., when I first had to face what it meant. Once I met her, once I had sorted through my marriage, sorted through my grief, my life, once it fit who she was and how she knew us, it was uncomplicated.

When she first walked up, it was shocking, awkward. With their physical similarities, she and my husband were related somehow, I knew, and then once I understood who she was, I realized that she was not only related but of him, a part of him. After I got over that, it just seemed like meeting a friend of a friend or finding someone who had come from the same hometown. Once I got through the surprise of hearing who she was, we settled in together, into some kind of relationship I'm not sure can be cleanly defined.

"You had every right to come," I said, wiping my mouth.

"I didn't ask you if I had a right," she responded quickly and then took a sip of coffee. "I asked you if you think I shouldn't have come." She was not letting it go.

I took a sip too, put down my cup, and placed both of my hands on the table.

"Lilly, you are a result of my husband's love. You are warm and kind, a woman who is a joy to be around. You and O.T. would have—" I stopped, not knowing how to say it. Then I made myself clear. "I am only sorry that you did not come sooner."

I took in a breath and ate some more of my pie. She faced me, smiled, and turned away.

"Maybe you won't want to hear this," she said shyly, "but you remind me of my mother."

I sat with her appraisal, her idea that these two women, connected by a man, her father, were somehow alike, somehow made from the same cloth. I let the words, the possibility, sift through the feelings and the memories that I had only recently allowed to surface, and I found that I was not offended or upset.

It would make sense that O.T. had found two comparable women to love. One when he was young and unbridled, the other when he was chained up, old inside. The idea that I bore some resemblance to the second woman my husband had cared for did not leave me bewildered or displeased. It was the same as having Lilly in my life, another wrinkle smoothed down.

"Do you think it's odd?" she asked.

"You mean about us or about O.T. and your mother?"

She shrugged her shoulders like she didn't know and ate another bite. "Everything, I guess." Then there was a pause. "What's it like for you?"

I wondered at her questions, if she really wanted to know what I thought or if she was just trying to find more proof that I was okay with her, that her coming didn't in some way break me or lessen my life with O.T.

"There's a lot," I replied, deciding how to tell her what place I had come to with all these things I now knew. I wasn't sure she would want to hear everything—how it was at first, the slight but sudden punch of betrayal, the struggle with anger and guilt, the immediate but then quickly released response of bitterness. I thought about her question and then answered as carefully as I could.

"My grandmother, my mother's mother," I added, "was a Navajo woman who married a Cherokee. Her name was Thelma Whitebead, but we often called her Grandma Cedar because she was strong and red like bark." I remembered how my mother had given her that name. As a child I had thought it was a perfect description of her. "When I was little she told me the story of the Spider Woman and how the Navajo women learned to weave."

I sat at my kitchen table and recalled the face of my grandmother when she told me this story. Her eyes narrowed, the lines around her mouth stiffened. She talked slower, her words like beats of a drum. She spoke as if the thing she was saying was the most important thing I would ever hear.

I turned to my husband's daughter, fully, and in the voice of my dead grandmother told her the tale from my childhood.

"There was a little girl who came upon a small hole in the ground as she was walking through the woods. As she peeked into the hole there was smoke rising from within. She moved closer. And when she examined what was inside, she saw an old woman weaving strands of thread with a wooden stick. She watched her and then asked her what she was doing. The woman replied that she was weaving a blanket."

Lilly was attentive, still.

"For three days the young girl stayed with the old woman and learned how to weave different designs into blankets. With each stitch, she followed the weaver's instructions, copied her, until she was able to make the same lovely blankets that the old woman was making.

"When the little girl had learned all that she needed to learn, the old woman said to her, 'Child, there is one warning I must give you, and you must pass this along to all those who weave these designs. Whenever you sew a blanket, you must make sure that you leave a hole in the middle. For if you do not, all of your weaving thoughts will be trapped in the stitches and will stay inside.'"

I remembered how my grandmother stretched her hands wide and slid her crooked fingers in and out of each other as she ended the storytelling.

I continued. "'It will not only bring you bad luck,' the old woman said, 'it will also make you crazy.' So when the little girl returned to her village and taught the others how to weave, she always remembered to share the old woman's warning. From that day on, my grandmother recounted, the Navajo leave a tiny hole in the middle of their blankets in obedience to the old Spider Woman's counsel."

Lilly nodded like she understood, but I knew I needed to explain.

"Since before I ever met O.T., your father," I said with respect, "I have been weaving a blanket, making my life. I am white and Cherokee, the child of a blind man and a sorrowing woman, the daughter of mountain people. All of this woven in me." I leaned closer to Lilly.

"I am the only child of my parents who lived. Three children, and I am the only one who survived. All of my family died before I was old enough to understand what it meant to be left alone. And I was so lonesome, so completely by myself, I even begged their spirits to stay with me." I sat back and remembered the house of my childhood, wondered if it was still full of the ghosts.

"And all that death and the loneliness was pulled like strands of cotton hard and taut into my heart."

I sat forward, resting my arms on the table.

"Even and especially when I could not have a child and then finally had one and she was born dead, I yanked and sewed and made this life of over seventy years."

I paused, now understanding what I had not for more than six decades.

"In all that time, in all that weaving, I did not leave a place for my pain to get out. I did not leave a hole like the old woman had said, like my grandmother had warned."

I stopped for a moment, to recollect, to make sure I

was saying it just right, to make sure I was understanding this for myself.

"Only once," I continued, recalling that night at the ocean, "did I ever let what I felt be released from me; only once did the seams that I had so carefully stitched together get pulled apart. And that happened only because I knew that if they didn't, I would fold up inside myself, smothering under the weight of such sorrow." I took a breath, that winter night at the beach a long, unforgotten moment in my life.

"Only once did I let the fear and the anger and the resentment and the sadness spill out of me. And even after I did that, I quickly sewed up the rip that had frayed and kept those feelings, that disappointment and grief, from ever slipping out again."

I stopped. I opened like a flower.

"My life has been so tight, so ordered and neatly sewn, that there was no room for O.T. to find what he needed. I shut him out. And I think that even though he was not loose with his emotions either, not one to deal with or talk about the things that burden a man, I think that somehow the love and the width of your mother's heart freed him, warmed him, eased him in a way that I could not."

I thought about O.T. and how painful it must have been for him to leave Clara. After Emma died and he came home, he was never the same again. He was a man engulfed in guilt, prepared to be punished because he believed that he was the cause of our daughter's death, that he alone, because of his infidelity, had stolen the breath of the baby his wife had wanted more than anything and then lost.

Surely, O.T. returned thinking that what he had done by loving another woman had produced seeds of evil, one single seed of disease that passed from him into our baby's heart, eventually spreading, multiplying itself into death. So that, because of his guilt, because of his lack of redemption, he put aside any thoughts of true love and replaced them with the regimen of devotion to the one to whom he was promised, the one he had so deeply invaded and wounded. He came home, extracted his need for attention, his desire for passion, and narrowed the size of his heart.

After Emma died, he stayed close to the farm, sending others to sales and fairs, and never allowed himself the pleasure of remembering how it had felt to be adored. All of what he had known from his two years with Clara, all of the little things he could not share with anyone but her, all of the simple silence and the romance and the deep, deep way he could sleep only next to her, he wrapped and packaged and put away. And he never again tampered with or peeked into the slender sleeve of love he had only briefly known.

I drew in another breath, waving off more thoughts of O.T. and how he suffered, and finished answering Lilly's question.

"So how am I doing with all of this? You want to know. What am I thinking?" I closed my eyes to consider the question more clearly, to make sure I was being as honest as I could be. I opened them and answered her as truthfully as I was able.

"I am trying to make a hole in my blanket, trying to

unhook the deeply made stitches, sew them together again around an opening that lets my heart release its contents. A hole, not a tear, not a rip or forced split this time. An intentional and purposely placed loop that pulls out all the pain and joy and fear and sadness and keeps it from being locked and hidden in tight hems ever again."

I paused.

"People look at me, my lack of anger at O.T. for having an affair, you and me, our friendship, and they may think it is odd or strange in some way. But that's not what is strange. Our relationship, my reaction— these things are not what is so out of the ordinary." I slid aside my cup of coffee.

"What is strange, what has been strange, is that with everything that has happened to me, the deaths, the loneliness, the hard choices, all of it, the oddest thing of it all is that I thought I could lock it away, put it out of reach, protect myself, and never deal with any of it. And that somehow as long as I didn't share it with anyone else, it would be forever harmless to me and everyone around me."

I reached my hands across the table toward Lilly.

"Your coming has opened me in a way I had not expected. And I don't understand it; it's you and it's not you. I can't explain it. But for whatever reason, your being here has allowed me, some might say forced me, but regardless, it has let me walk again across the paths of my life and see who I have become, feel what has happened to me, understand who I am."

Rays of late afternoon sun flooded through the

window, and I suddenly felt warmed.

"You have done what my parents, my siblings, my grandmother, my daughter, their spirits, my husband were never fully able to do. You let me remember and feel the deep and burdened things that have been inside me, cluttered and undisturbed for most of my life. You let me remember and feel them, and then you let me see that I would not die because of it. You have helped me grieve all the death that has always surrounded me. You have brought me permission to be in touch with my heart."

We sat in a long, unbothered span of silence before either of us spoke.

"You know," Lilly said finally and matter-of-factly, "Mama would have liked you." She laughed, the thought of saying such a thing surprising her. "And even though she would have thought it was peculiar that you and I could be friends and she probably would never have said so, she would have liked that too."

I smiled at her and nodded my head, the thought of her mother's approval, like the early evening sunlight, an unexpected delight.

I settled again into my place at the table and realized what I enjoyed most about my husband's daughter. She was, in ways I had never experienced, truthful. She spoke without restraint.

We finished our pie quietly, without further conversation, bathing in the dazzling pink light of the setting sun. We said nothing else to each other, and I understood that, unlike the days of my early life, everything that needed to be had, in fact, already been said.

135

17

Maude flies into the house. It is well into the month of May, past early spring, brilliant. A world melting into soft color.

"Your water," she is yelling at me while I walk toward her, still in my pajamas, from the bedroom. "Your water is clear, blue!"

She is frantic, full of her own news.

I go over to the window and open the curtains. Daffodils and orange-red tulips line the walkway. The morning sky is wide and undisturbed. I yawn and move toward the kitchen. "Coffee?" I ask.

"Decaffeinated?" She follows in behind me.

"Yeah, I can do that," I reply, wondering why I allow her to change my morning routine. I pull the bag out from behind several plastic canisters in the cabinet.

Then I stop and think for a minute whether I had locked the door last night. "How did you get in here?"

She is sitting at the table, sticking her finger in my African violet, checking to see if it needs water. "The key above the door frame in the garage," she answers.

"You went out to my garage and took the key and let yourself in?" I ask, surprised at her boldness.

"Sure," she says. "I did it a lot when you stayed with O.T." She wipes her fingers on a paper towel. "You did tell me where it was and asked me to check on things," she says, like I invited her in this morning.

"That was only if you thought it was important," I reply, pouring the water in the top of the coffeemaker.

"Well, it always was." And then as if she suddenly remembered why she is here, she adds, "And this is even more so." She comes over to the sink next to me and washes her hands.

"Last night I dreamed about you." She searches around for a towel. "You were so beautiful," she says, like it could only happen in a dream.

Then she sits down again.

"The water after I saw your face was like from a waterfall."

The coffeemaker starts to drip and I take out two cups. I listen.

"It wasn't motionless, still, like a pond or a lake. It was," she stops and turns toward the living room window, where the sun is shining through making slender white lines across the wall. "It was moving like a mountain stream or brook." She seems so pleased with herself.

"Like a creek?" I ask, feeling as if I had the same dream.

"A clean one," she answers, "not like what we have now."

I sit down next to her and begin to remember.

"Is there red clay on one side, granite rock and moss on the other?"

She stares at me, stunned. She nods.

"And as you go along is there a large tree, an oak or elm, a big one, growing crooked and leaning across the creek, its branches almost reaching the other side?"

She is entranced. "And cold," she replies. "Mostly it is cold."

137

"Except where the sun is not hidden," I finish her sentence. "There is a spot, no bigger than this room, where the sun is strong and unblocked."

Maude nods slowly at me.

"And that is where the water is the clearest, where you can see the pebbles, shining like silver, where you can find crayfish and tiny white eggs," I say as I turn away. My face feels flushed, hot.

I get up and pour us coffee. We wait in the silence.

"I used to go to a place like that when I was young." I sit down in the chair opposite my neighbor. "It was the only time, after moving away from the mountain, where I felt like I was home."

Maude is alert, on the edge of her seat, listening.

"O.T.'s brother and I used to sneak out there after we fed the horses."

I remember the way we walked and then ran, all the time telling each other that his mother was inside making beds and cleaning up breakfast dishes, unable to see us.

"It was our secret place," I say, shyly.

Maude, totally uncharacteristic, is quiet.

"He never tried anything, if that's what you think," I say, in defense of both of our honor.

She shakes her head like she hadn't considered such a possibility and gets up for some milk.

I gaze outside and into the sun. I notice the lawn. The grass is tall and bending.

"Only once did we touch." I take the carton from her and pour a little into my cup.

She waits to hear more.

I am surprised at how easily I tell the story. "There was this community picnic, some big event that every-body attended. There was music and games. Maybe it was July Fourth or something." I am trying to think of the date but then I realize it doesn't matter.

"But after a couple of hours I left because I was bored with the people and the conversation. It was mostly Witherspoon family stuff or talk about the war; and since I was not interested in that great American history lesson, I left. I went to that sunny place by the creek, slid off my shoes, dropped the hem of my skirt in the water, and stood there in the clearest, warmest part."

I remember how it felt, the sudden surprise of smooth stones rolling under my feet, the refreshing way the water flowed by me.

"He was already there, waiting for me, he said."

I smile, thinking how right it seemed, how the sun was not too hot, the creek not too cold, the easy way he reached down from the fat limb of the old leaning tree and pulled me into it. How it felt to be so close to him, finally, dangerous and innocent both at the same time.

I think about how my heart was beating so fast I had to turn away and catch my breath.

"He only brushed his fingers across my cheek. That was all." I take a sip of my coffee and then close my eyes, remembering his touch.

"And when I faced him, fully prepared to be kissed or held or do whatever he asked, whatever he wanted, he just looked away, waited for what seemed an eternity, jumped down, and then helped me out of the tree."

I remember the day as if it were yesterday. The

shadow of disappointment that hung across his face, the soft sadness in his eyes. He picked up our shoes and slung them over his shoulders, and together we walked out of the creek and up the road to join the others, neither of us sure what had just happened between us, what it meant or what we would ever do with it.

"And that was the closest we ever came to being lovers." I get up from the table and pull out a box of cereal.

Maude responds. "It's weird, don't you think, that I would have had this dream based on your memories? Do you think it means something?" Her voice is inquisitive.

I shrug my shoulders.

My neighbor keeps working it out. "I mean, do you think that now that you know about O.T. and that woman and everything, that maybe you wish something more would have happened that day?"

She pauses. She's so sure there's something to this.

"Do you think the water is clear at the place of this memory because you now know that what you've really desired, what you really always wished for, is that you had been his lover? And that you've always wanted that and regretted that it didn't happen?" She is measuring my life, ordering my memories.

"And now because you know that O.T. was messing around you finally don't have to feel guilty anymore." She exhales a puff of air like an exclamation point. She is so pleased with herself.

My back is to my neighbor as I reach for my breakfast. I realize that she cannot see my face, read my thoughts, so I turn to her so as not to hide anything.

"Maude, it isn't some child's game. I haven't lived my life counting out marbles or coins, only to make sure my husband doesn't get more than I do. I live with what I got, what I have chosen, what I let go of, what I've held to the tightest. There isn't any keeping score or way to make things even, in love or in suffering, in life."

I lift my eyes to see beyond the room, out the door she has left wide and open. Everything outside is alive.

I redirect my focus to her. She stirs sugar in her coffee.

"In the end, it isn't how you count things that matters, it's how the things that matter count."

I sit down at the table with my breakfast and put the box of cereal and a clean bowl in front of her.

She reaches out and taps me on the hand, nodding in approval as if she knew my feelings all along. Her prophecies solid and truthful.

"Then it's certain." She is radiant, self-assured. "There is nothing odd," she says, "about how I see your water."

She smiles at me with complete confidence. Then she checks the expiration date on the carton of milk, breathes a sigh of great relief, and pours all that is left for herself.

She is intense, forthright, and even beautiful.

"The trouble has finally passed," she states, boldly and with authority, like she is rendering a pronouncement of pardon, like all of the mysteries of my life have been solved. Like there is nothing left unknown.

Acknowledgments

I gratefully acknowledge the continued support and friendship I receive from my agent, Sally McMillan, and my editor, Renee Sedliar. I'd be lost without their guidance.

I am thankful to be included on the HarperSanFrancisco list.

I am especially indebted to manuscript editor Priscilla Stuckey; production editor Lisa Zuniga; publicists Roger Freet, Laina Adler, and Jennifer Johns; and friend Sam Barry.

The Russian fable comes from *I Wanted the Elevator But I Got the Shaft,* Joe G. Emerson (Nashville, TN: Dimensions for Living, 1993), and much of the information about the Indian Removal Act as well as the Navajo Spiderwoman weaving story come from *Through Indian Eyes* (Pleasantville, NY: Reader's Digest, 1997).

I acknowledge, with gratitude, the stories I learned about dreams from Addie Luther and about education in the mountains of North Carolina from Mrs. Ruth McRae.

I also wish to thank my husband, Bob Branard, who has never, not once since I told him my dream, ever doubted I would be published.

I am a lucky woman.

Center Point Publishing
600 Brooks Road ● PO Box 1
Thorndike ME 04986-0001 USA

(207) 568-3717

US & Canada:
1 800 929-9108